MW00398872

"...is enthralling. When a local schoolteacher is murdered, family values and ethical choices clash in this small Eastern Oregon town. The Wade family, having only recently moved to Baker City, unwillingly becomes deeply involved in solving the murder. I highly recommend this book."

Betty Kuhl, Betty's Books, Baker City, Oregon

"...is a clear cut above much of the mystery genre with its fine period detail and its clean, fast-moving narrative. Like Harper Lee, Wright explore[s] much of what makes real tragedy in our lives: the violence of memory, the loss of innocent perspective, the fractured trust in intimate relationships and our human tendency to reduce what threatens us into simplistic and often erroneous interpretations."

Barbara J. Scot, New York Times Notable Author
of *A Prairie Reunion* and *Stations at Still Creek*

"...is a fascinating trip through the psyche of a young boy as he struggles to understand a very adult world... Wright evokes simpler times in simpler places, yet this story is anything but simple. I found it enjoyable and...with the insights of a writer at home with his material."

Loretta Stinson, Graduate Editor
Portland State University Publishing Program

"...brings back the simple days of an Eastern Oregon boyhood, along with things which are not so simple—murder, suspicion, and family loyalty. Highly readable."

Nicole Mones, author of *Lost in Translation* and *A Cup of Light*

Baker City 1948

a novel

Books by
George Byron Wright

FICTION

Baker City 1948

NONFICTION

The Not-For-Profit CEO:
A Survivor's Manual

Beyond Nominating:
A Guide to Gaining and
Sustaining Successful
Not-For-Profit Boards

To Janice Kennedy!

Baker City 1948

a novel

George Byron Wright (signature)

George Byron Wright

C3 Publications
Portland, Oregon
www.c3publication.com

Baker City 1948
Copyright ©2005 by George Byron Wright.

C3 Publications
3495 NW Thurman Street
Portland, OR 97210-1283
www.c3publications.com

First Edition

ISBN 0-9632655-2-0
ISBN 978-0-9632655-2-4
Library of Congress Control Number: 2005907477

Cataloging References: Baker City 1948
   1. Oregon-fiction 2. Baker City, OR 3. Period-1948
   4. Murder-fiction 5. Family-boys-fiction 6. Title

Book and jacket design by Dennis Stovall, Red Sunsets, Inc.

Cover photo courtesy of Oregon Trail Regional Museum, Baker City, Oregon.

Printed in the United States of America.

"A man does what he must—in spite of personal consequences, in spite of obstacles and dangers and pressures—and that is the basis of all morality."

—John F. Kennedy

In Memory of
Catherine Elizabeth Douglass
1882–1948

Acknowledgements

First, thanks to my parents, George Baxter and Eleanor Wright, who gave my brother Paul and me the experience of living in the small towns of Oregon. Otherwise, this novel would have had no basis in reality. They live on in my memory.

After gracious first readers, and many revisions, I was blessed to gain the sage advice and counsel of Dennis Stovall, Director of Ooligan Press and Coordinator of the Publishing Curriculum at Portland State University. He is also the designer of the cover and text format. Thanks as well to Karen Kirtley, Portland State University editing instructor, and to her class of spring 2005, for editing this novel as a class project. What an exhilarating experience, having 15 editors at once. Alan Dubinsky served admirably as the final line editor.

My first readers took on the raw first draft and came back to me with support and critical input. Thanks to: Michael Hosokawa, Cynthia Griffin, John Wykoff, Helen Kennedy, Jennifer Boyd and Greg Nokes.

Since this novel is set in 1948, I had to do some research in Baker City. I owe a debt of gratitude to two institutions for helping me get my facts straight. The Baker County Library is a wonderful facility and has held fast to its historical treasures for which

I am grateful, especially the newspaper microfilm files and city directories collection. The Oregon Trail Regional Museum's photographic collection yielded the photo of Baker City's Main Street, circa 1947, which is used on the cover.

A special note of thanks to several Baker City folks who helped me in my research: Gary and Eloise Dielman, Chary Mires, and Melissa Shafer; all of whom were expert and gracious with their assistance.

Thanks to Sidney Lezak, a specialist in mediation and former long-serving U.S. Attorney for Oregon, for his insights into the legal system and its vagaries in 1948. As is the case with all of those who advised me, I take full credit for any discrepancies or inaccuracies.

Of course, the one person who has lived through every revision, every trip to Baker City, and read every new version is my wife, Betsy. Her unwavering encouragement and faith is a special gift.

George B. Wright
Portland, Oregon
August 2005

Author's Note: The town was named Baker City from 1866 to 1911, when it was changed to simply Baker to sound more cosmopolitan. It was renamed Baker City in 1989. Even though this novel is set in 1948, the author has chosen to use the name Baker City for purposes of currency and literary license.

— 1 —

As a boy, I knew nothing of the dark memory that my father had carried like some parasite since his youth—at least I didn't for a long time. Then in 1947, shortly after my eighth birthday, my father decided to become a mortician. One year later, he embalmed his first dead body for pay, but not before he had uprooted our family and orchestrated our displacement. Soon afterward there was a killing in this new place we had come to, and the circumstances of that horror unleashed something in my father, turning it loose on him and on us. Did he do a noble thing? I still wonder, and that is what compels me to put it all down here.

In any event, we were going to live someplace else. I didn't know that people did that. Being eight, I assumed that where you were, was where you would be, period. But sure enough, in the chill of January in 1948 we vacated the big house on Twelfth Street, left my birthplace—The Dalles, Oregon, on the banks of the mighty Columbia—and rode the Union Pacific Streamliner to a place called Baker City. My father, Kenneth Longworth Wade, former longshoreman and World War II veteran, was about to become a funeral director and embalmer.

Deep into the night, the train powered down, coasted into Baker City, and ground to a stop, the diesels surging impatiently. It was so black out that my little brother, David, and I, groggy from a fitful slumber, saw only our own reflections in the dark glass of the coach window. We were the only passengers to get off, left standing beneath a dim station light as the train growled away and vanished through a black curtain. The depot was locked. Nothing moved. I could hear the sound of my own breathing in the cold air. I guessed that we weren't expected. Felt like that. The only sound was the squeak of the phone booth accordion door. My father stood under the dome light, thumbed at the directory that hung from a chain, and plugged a nickel into the slot. Shortly, an old Chevrolet lumbered up. It had "Eight-0 Taxi" painted in white letters on its doors. Come to find out, all of the taxis in Baker City were named with a number: The "Eight-0," the "One Twenty-One," and the "Thirteen" taxis. The driver nodded when my father told him where we wanted to go. He wrestled our luggage into the trunk and, without smile or comment, drove us through the dark to 1440 Elm Street. The moving van was waiting for us there with its slumbering driver, an unpleasant man who stumbled from the truck's cab and stood scowling and knuckling his eyes.

The house, so memorable now, was merely a dark outline that night—black on blacker, an unfamiliar silhouette squatting in the cold with chunks of clotted snow scattered around it. That night, David and I took to the house as we found her because without her we were homeless.

My mother stood guard while my father and the sullen van driver completed our migration, grunting and hefting and swaying under boxes and beds and the prized cedar chest and the revered piano. In the wee hours we fell into our familiar beds, smelled our own pillows, and slept quick and hard. My last thought before sleep came was *Where am I?*

We had been made off with, David and I—dumped into a strange new place and given but a few hours of sleep before our mother force-marched us to register for school the very next day. Facing twenty pairs of prying, suspicious eyes at Tiedemann Elementary School proved to be the most unnerving part of moving to a new town. That, and being slobbered over by Miss Carmalita Bunn, who towered over me wearing a tent of a dress, emblazoned with huge white and red flowers. When she leaned down, a fog of perfume cauterized my nostrils, and when she spoke, spittle sprayed onto my face; it was, indeed, horrifying. I could only yearn for Miss Fitzgerald, the beautiful, young, red-haired teacher I'd left behind. The trade was inhumane.

But ready or not, we began life at 1440. In 1948, Baker City's population was right around 9,400 in an area less than six miles square. But my immediate world was mostly the tramping ground radiating out from our house, about six blocks out and back. Two blocks south stood Freddie Patterson's Grocery where I spent a lot of time reading comics I didn't buy. Between our house and Freddie's lived an elderly third cousin of my father. Chester Stillman, a bear of a man with massive hands gnarled from years of working for the railroad, and Ruth, his peppery wife, became immediate family.

Most fascinating to me was the stub of ground across the highway from our house called Old Reservoir Hill. It was the highest point in town, and while it no longer served as a reservoir, I soon found out that an earthen and wood-beam tunnel ran through the hill ready-made for heroic exploration. Two blocks to the rear of 1440 ran the murky waters of the Powder River made muddy by the Sumpter Dredge still clawing for gold ore upriver. David and I would spend hours reconnoitering the riverbank and the dense trees and brush along its edge.

That is until we discovered the shack.

- 2 -

The day David and I stumbled across the building, secreted in among the trees, we'd been at the river throwing rocks and just knocking around. It was on a sunny Saturday morning as I remember and surprisingly mild for mid-February, one of those languid moments that a boy enjoys without noting that he is. At some point, we postponed the tossing of stone missiles and wandered back through the brushy trees and brown winter grass—nothing on our minds, nothing demanding anything of us.

We were picking our way through the trees and the undergrowth, slashing with the green switches we had broken off a sapling, when we came up on a small wooden building. We'd never seen the squat, tar-papered shack before. It just materialized, a secret place out of nowhere. Tendrils of smoke snaked out of a rusted stovepipe. We squatted down; I shushed David. A man's face suddenly filled a dirty windowpane and stared out at us with unblinking black-dot eyes then drew back. In an instant, the shack's door squawked open. The man sprang out and stood spraddle-legged staring at us. I guessed him to be about my father's age. He had thick black hair, heavy eyebrows, and wore a wrinkled, blue and white flannel shirt and some sort of heavy olive green pants held up by black suspenders.

"What you doing here?" His hands were fisted on his hips.

"Nothing," I said. "We're not doing nothing."

He shoved his hands into his pockets and took a couple steps toward us. For a long moment he studied me, then David. I took a step back, pulling David with me, thinking that maybe he meant to grab us.

"You kids live around here?" His voice was unfamiliar and hard.

I tilted my head. "Back that way—up on Elm Street."

He spit a stream of brown juice like I'd seen my uncle Steve do. "What are your names?"

"I'm Philip, he's David." David's eyes were wide, staring out from beneath the fur band of his imitation leather aviator's helmet.

"You got a last name?"

"Wade," I said.

The man stood quiet and ran a hand through his thick hair. "You boys ought not to be down here. River's dangerous."

"You live here?" I asked right out. "In that place?"

He turned and looked at the shack, then back at me, a short smile creasing his face. "Yep. This here's home sweet home for me, boys."

"Don't you have a real house?" David blurted out.

"This is it." The man frowned, and David shrank against me. "I like it down here. It's peaceful, and I got my privacy—people usually leave me alone."

"Don't you like people?" I asked.

"No. People are mostly looking out for themselves." He pulled down on his suspenders as he spoke and turned to stare off at the river and was quiet. A moment later, he broke off his gaze and walked back to the cabin, but stopped at the corner and looked at us again.

"You boys, just move on now." He pulled the shack's door open and stood quietly, looking at the ground. "It's best you don't come back. This is where I live, and I don't want folks around. Now go on home."

"What's your name, mister?" I asked.

He shook his head. "Never mind," he said frowning. "I'm not going to say it again—get on out of here." He waved his arm.

We snaked back through the brush and didn't stop until we got home.

David and I sat on the back steps, beads of perspiration on our pink faces, and stared back toward the river. When we'd caught our breath, we rushed into the house and confronted our mother, who had her hands up to her wrists in raw hamburger. She listened patiently to our breathless telling of the encounter with the black-haired, black-eyed man. At first she listened with one ear before her instincts kicked in. At that moment, she took her hands out of the hamburger and cracker crumbs and asked us to repeat our tale. After the second telling, she sat on a kitchen chair and made us stand in front of her. I could see the alarm in her eyes.

"Now listen to me," she began, "you boys are not to go down there, to…to wherever this person is. Don't go near that place. Understand?"

"Why not?" David asked. "I like it down there."

"Because, David, we have no idea who that man is or what he's doing down there. No arguments. Stay away from there, you hear me now?"

"Who do you think he is, Mom?" I asked.

"I have no idea, but I don't like it. I'll talk with your father when he gets home."

After a final admonishment to stay put, my mother went back

to her meatloaf and waited until the man of the house was home to unleash her anxieties.

In 1948 my father was 37 years old. He was just a tad under six feet tall, heavyset, but not fat, with black hair that had been thinning since his early twenties, gold-rimmed glasses framing brown eyes, and a handsome face that always looked more full and oval than he liked. His private passion, his necessity even, was poetry; it was a familiar sight to see my father, pad and pencil in hand, his face a map of concentration, jotting down short lines of cursive verse. I came to understand that writing poetry was his attempt to override the limits life held him to.

To see my parents together was to witness severe contrasts. Kenneth Longworth carried pigmentation that granted him the blessings of the sun; he tanned with ease, while Margaret Louise, fair of skin to the point of alabaster, could take no sun. My mother blue of eye and my father brown eyed, his black hair contrasting her auburn. Kenneth's jovial nature was offset by Margaret's modesty. My father's artistic talents were large, but he never tested them to the fullest. My mother was a person of moderate creative potential, but she mastered the piano to the maximum of her workmanlike skills.

≡✶

That Saturday afternoon my father calmly walked home from the mortuary with the *Democrat-Herald* tucked under one arm, only to be met by a she-bear. As my father leaned over to kiss my mother, she waved him off and began spitting out the story of the mystery man.

"Good heavens, Ken, there's no telling what kind of man is hiding out down there," she said, raising a hand to her forehead. "Makes my blood run cold."

My father listened quietly, kissed my mother on the cheek, and gave me a wink and ruffled my hair. "Quite a day, Philip." He unrolled the paper and studied the headlines. "Well, I don't think I'll call the police just yet. What say I stroll down there and take a look, instead?"

My father changed out of his suit into his chore clothes and walked down the dirt road toward the river. I started after him, only to be motioned back with a wave of his hand. All I could do was watch until he left the road and disappeared into the trees.

I went back inside. What if my father got hurt? Had my mother thought of that? She was going right on fixing dinner like nothing unusual was happening. She directed me to set the table and pour the milk. I did but my mind was on the river and what was happening down there. Every few minutes, I would go out on the back porch and look down the road, only to have my mother call me back.

After what seemed like hours, I saw my father swinging up the road in that splayed walk he had—feet thrown out to the side in an exaggerated stride—and ran to meet him, looking for wounds or blood. He was all in one piece, even smiling. He put his arm around my shoulder when I got to him.

"Nice down by the river," he said in a calm voice. "First time I've been down there. Really nice."

"Did you see him? The man in the shack?" I asked.

"Yes."

"What happened? Was he mad?"

"No, he wasn't mad." He kept walking and patted me on the back.

"What'd he say, Dad? Did he tell you to get away from there too?"

He squeezed my shoulder. "No, it wasn't like that, son. Let's us wait to talk about it. Your mother's holding a hot meal."

I was dying to hear about the man in the shack, but our dinnertime code stipulated that family things came first. I messed with my food and waited through a letter from Grandma Brownman, which her daughter dutifully read aloud. Then we listened to my father's account of *directing* his first funeral, whatever that meant. The black-eyed man stirred in my head while my father spoke calmly of a family's misfortune, as he called it—of a ranching accident and a son who *was taken* from them, a family name of McKay.

"What's a misfortune, Dad?" David asked, picking at his green beans.

My father pulled on an ear lobe, thought for a moment, then said, "Well, it's something that makes people unhappy. Like when you pinched your finger in the door, remember?" He did. "Sometimes it's even more hurtful than that."

"Dad, what about the man at the river?" I broke in, tired of pointless talk.

He considered me, nodded, and leaned on his elbows. "All right. Yes, the shack was there, just like you said."

"And this person the boys described, he actually lives there?" my mother asked.

"Yep. He was sitting in the doorway when I came up on the building."

"He was mean to us," David said, tilting his head forward for emphasis.

"Was he mean to you, Dad?"

"No, David. He wasn't. Name's Jack O'Brien—said he remembered you boys."

"Well, I don't like it," my mother said. "What's he doing down there? Scaring children. Makes my skin crawl to think of someone skulking around in the trees."

My father took a bite of hominy. "Doubt he's that sinister. Just living there, Margaret. That little one-room shack."

"I don't care, he could be dangerous. We ought to notify the authorities."

"No, don't think that's called for. He's not hurting anybody I know of. We talked a bit. He's a veteran. Served in the Philippines."

"Can't see why he'd pick Baker City to be a bum in," my mother said.

"'Cause he's from around here. Grew up in Huntington, 50 miles south. Father died when he was a teenager. He enlisted in the army right out of high school."

"I don't like it," my mother said again. "I won't have a moment's peace thinking about that man down there and the boys out playing. Surely, he has family. Why isn't he with them, for heaven's sake?"

"That came up." My father nodded. "Has no kin around here. Just an older brother in California, but they don't speak. Guess while Jack was in the service, his brother talked their mother into selling the family acreage and moving to California near him. The man came home to nothing. Had it out with the brother about cheating him and got a few thousand dollars for his troubles. With that and a small military disability pension, he gets by."

My mother was shaking her head again. "Strange. How did you get him to talk so much?"

"Just hit it off, I guess. I think he's kind of lonely down there, no matter what he says to the contrary. But he's definitely a loner.

When he was done talking with me, he just went back inside and shut the door. Left me standing there with my face hanging out."

It was agreed among our family to leave the man alone. My father found out that that piece of land by the river was owned by the city. The public works crew knew about Jack O'Brien squatting in the old tool shed. There were a good number of veterans among their number who chose to look the other way and leave the man alone.

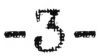

Whenever it rained that winter, or when snow melted on the roof, water the color of tea would dribble from the ceiling in the kitchen directly over the table and in the living room just in front of the Zenith radio. David and I were pressed into duty as the official coffee can patrol. We thought it was neat, but plinking tin didn't charm my mother.

At the worst of the leaking, my father decided that he would put a new roof on 1440 himself. It couldn't be all that difficult, he reasoned, and in the face of my mother's doubt he said, "I can do it, Margaret." For David and me, it would be welcome commotion. That roof looked very high and scary, but I couldn't wait to see my father look down at us from such a dizzying height. I didn't know then what courage it really took for him to climb up there—that he was terrified of heights and that only the family's burdensome financial circumstances drove him up that ladder.

That's when Jack O'Brien came back into our lives—as cheap labor—despite my mother's opposition.

Late on a Friday afternoon in April, a flatbed truck from Eardley Lumber & Building Supplies rumbled up our side street stirring up a swirl of dust. Two wiry young men with nothing much to say jumped out and off-loaded rolls of tar paper and dark green composition roofing, along with a box of roofing nails and a bucket of tar patch. Early the next morning, with the sun warming a cloudless sky, my mother rose and prepared my father a hearty breakfast of pancakes and eggs, which he dutifully ate. Then he kissed her on the cheek and went out to slay his dragon. David and I were right on his heels when he and Jack O'Brien met out in the yard, shook hands and looked up at our roof—talking, nodding, arms folded.

The two men were still deciding how to tackle the job when Uncle Chet Stillman's gray Plymouth pulled up beside the yard with a wooden extension ladder roped to the roof. Uncle Chet swung a suicide door open and emerged in an awkward twisting motion, favoring his damaged back, and limped over to my father and Jack O'Brien with a wide smile on his face.

"Well, boys," Uncle Chet said, "it's a fine day for me to watch you two crawling around on that roof."

My father's mouth spread into an uneasy smile. "Damn, Chet, I just want to get this done without falling to my death."

"Well, if it comes to that, I know a good funeral home."

"Very funny." My father turned to Jack O'Brien, who was standing to the side, waiting. "Chet, meet Jack O'Brien. Jack, this is Chet Stillman, a questionable relation of mine."

The two men stepped in, leaned a bit at the waist, and did the *nice to meet you* business with a quick, hard handshake and nod.

With Uncle Chet sitting in the yard on one of our kitchen chairs and David and me watching the high wire act, my father and Jack O'Brien put a new roof on 1440. It wasn't an artistic achievement, but it never leaked. They slathered black goo on the worst spots, patched over some places with tar paper, then rolled the new asphalt roofing covered with dark green grit right over the old roofing. It was the cheapest and quickest way to do the job.

Sweat glistened on my father's round face. From time to time, he would pause and wipe his face on the tail of his white tee shirt, then push up his glasses and continue on. Once or twice he slipped on the steep incline, and my heart jumped. Uncle Chet seemed to know just what to say on those occasions.

"No dancing allowed up there, Ken. City ordinance."

My father would flap a hand at him and go on, his face a grim mask.

Jack O'Brien was a horse. Early on, he shed his shirt, revealing a lean, muscular body. His body also glistened with sweat, but it seemed to radiate from strength and certainty, as opposed to my father's less confident actions. Jack O'Brien sprang up the ladder. My father took each step like a man condemned, but I was proud of him even as he struggled.

Then it was finished, the job capped off. As dusk settled in, my father and Jack O'Brien carried the remnants down the ladder—one last trip. Finished and fatigued, they stepped quietly back into the yard and looked up. David and I stood beside them. It was a moment of reverence. The air was still, and the light dimmed as evening approached.

The two men admired their work for a couple of minutes then shook hands, and Jack O'Brien stayed for dinner. My father had won the debate over having the man at our table. It seemed odd to have this particular stranger in our house. He asked to wash up and emerged freshly scrubbed, wet hair slicked back and the sleeves of his plaid shirt rolled up on his forearms. His hands were clean, but the day's dirty work had left a residue of roofing grit beneath his nails.

When Jack O'Brien sat next to me, he smelled different than my father did when he worked hard. It was a musky scent, both strange and pleasurable.

My mother had fixed a fine meal and, I am sure, stretched the family food budget. Jack O'Brien and my father ate hungrily and quickly, as if to complete the cycle, conclude their brief alliance, and put things back the way they were. After a healthy piece of my mother's yellow cake with thick chocolate icing, topped off with a cup of coffee, Jack O'Brien slid his chair back and smiled at her.

"Miz Wade, I haven't had a meal like that in a spell. Reminds me of home and regular sit-down meals. I'm most appreciative."

"Thank you, Mr. O'Brien," she said. "We're most appreciative in return for your help."

"Don't mention it."

My father scooted his chair back. "Jack, what say we take care of business before you head home?"

Jack O'Brien nodded and followed my father into the kitchen. We heard the mumbling of the men's voices, then the screen door opened and clapped back. A few moments later, my father re-joined us and said nothing more about the man who had eaten at our table.

"Well, I'm glad that's over," he said, stretching his arms and flexing his shoulders. "I'm bushed." He leaned down and kissed his wife on the cheek. "Thanks. Great meal. I'm going to take a hot bath and go straight to bed."

I only saw Jack O'Brien one more time in my life.

– 4 –

May 24, 1948. I remember that date like no other. By the time David and I got up, our Zenith console radio, with its eerily glowing green eye, was already on. We were used to its familiar background of music and news interspersed with commercials for a new Buick or Rexall Drug Store jingles. We dressed to the radio's drone. We ate breakfast to it. It was the fifth member of our family. KBKR Radio gave us snippets of news and the popular music of the day.

That morning we were eating breakfast in the kitchen like any other day. The Andrews Sisters were singing *Rum and Co-ca-Cola*. David and I toyed with soggy cereal and gulped orange juice. My mother was making a second round of toast and spreading gooey margarine on it, the kind you mixed in a plastic bag by popping a yellow pill and squeezing it until the white stuff turned yellow.

My father was finishing a cup of coffee and taking one more look at the previous evening's *Democrat-Herald* when his head suddenly snapped up as if it were on a fishing line. He patted the air with this hand, shushed us, shoved his chair back so hard it fell over backward, and rushed into the living room with us boys in hot pursuit, suddenly not groggy anymore. Our mother soon followed, holding a table knife in one hand and looking quizzically after her husband.

"Ken, what is it?"

Again, he pawed the air with one hand and leaned on the Zenith with the other. "To repeat," came the nasal voice of the announcer, "a local schoolteacher was found brutally murdered last night, according to Baker City Police Chief, Howard Wisdom. The body of Katherine Elaine Dugan, age 46, a second-grade teacher at Tiedemann Elementary School, was found around 10:30 p.m. last evening by three Baker City boys off River Drive near the bank of the Powder River. There are no known suspects at this time, according to Chief Wisdom. The body is in the custody of County Coroner, Arthur Woodhull. KBKR will keep our listeners informed as additional details become known."

My father snapped off the radio and turned to his wife as the green eye dimmed to black. "My lord," he said. Mother's eyes opened wide; she stood stark still and held tightly to the butter knife, which had a glob of margarine clinging to its tip. My parents stared at one another for a silent moment before my father shook off his daze and said, "Well, I'd better get over there. Arthur and Sam will have their hands full."

Mrs. Dugan. I knew who she was. Her classroom was right across from that of Carmalita Bunn, my fourth-grade drill sergeant. The formidable Miss Bunn towered over her students like a monolith, but Mrs. Dugan was shorter, petite, and much prettier, and she actually smiled at us. At Tiedemann, teachers took turns greeting students each morning as they came to school. It always made me feel good when Mrs. Dugan was the first face I saw. Her smile made me smile.

I tried to imagine that someone I knew—a person so alive and wonderful—could have something so awful happen to her. I couldn't. *Brutally* and *murdered* were just words to me. Nothing more.

My father was finishing the Windsor knot on his tie. My mother stood in the bedroom doorway, hands clasped beneath her chin, staring at the floor, while we boys hovered in the hallway.

"You don't suppose they're going to have school today do you?" she asked.

My father kept wrapping the tie and stuffed it down into the waiting loop.

"I have no idea," he said, distracted and focused.

My mother walked into the bedroom, turned around and came back to the doorway. "Well, for heavens sake, Ken, this story is all over town by now. The children and their parents have heard that something bad has happened to one of their teachers."

My father yanked the tie through and cinched up the knot under the starched collar. "Margaret, children are more resilient than we think. To disrupt their routine would create more anxiety than just going on as usual."

He took his suit coat off the bed and slipped it on.

"I'm just not sure what to do about the boys," my mother said. "Should I call the school?"

My father pulled his shirt cuffs down to show beneath his coat sleeves, peered out into the hall at us, then back at my mother. "Don't call the school. The last thing they need over there is more phone calls. Just send the boys on as usual. If the principal and superintendent have decided not to hold classes, they'll send them home. The least they'll get is a nice walk on a sunny day. Not a bad tradeoff considering."

My mother looked down at us for a long moment, then gathered up a weak smile. "All right, boys. Finish dressing and I'll fix your lunches."

The air bristled with excitement. I *wanted* to go to school.

I started to get my jacket but was stopped by my mother's hushed voice. "You know, Ken, she is...was the same Katherine Dugan who attended our church and sang in the choir." My mother had been recruited as church pianist almost from the moment we first attended Baker Community Church.

I stopped to listen.

"No. I hadn't realized that," my father said. "In the choir?"

"Yes."

Another pause. "Then, you must have seen her every week at choir practice."

"Yes. She was an accomplished soprano." My mother's voice lurched and ended with a sob. She covered her mouth with both hands and closed her eyes tightly.

I held my place in the doorway and watched. Until that moment, when I saw my mother's face wrinkle into a mask of grief, I had been caught up in childish enthusiasm—something exciting had happened, something to change everyday predictability. Seeing my mother's sadness shamed me.

She spoke again, her voice shaking. "Katherine was really a lovely person.

I can't imagine that she's gone—or why someone would..."

"I know." My father held her tightly for a long moment, then kissed her gently on the forehead. She dabbed her eyes with a tissue, gave him a brave smile, and brushed at something invisible on his suit coat.

My father saw me watching. He stepped over and took me by

the shoulders.

"Philip, you and David go on to school. If they aren't having classes today, you two boys are to come right back here—directly. I don't want your mother to worry. She needs to know where you are. Understand?"

I nodded.

He squeezed my shoulders very firmly—I got the message.

"Fine," he said. "Well, I must get over there, Margaret. I'll call." She nodded and sniffed one more time and blew gently into her tissue.

≡☆

I burst out the front door that morning. David called for me to wait up. We didn't dawdle at the bridge or kick rocks in Lew Brothers parking lot, nearly running all the way to school. But we did hold up at Woodhull's Funeral Home and look at it like it might explode at any moment. We saw it every day, but that morning it felt like the big white house was staring back at us, as if it knew something we didn't. Each window was a glassy eye.

We were well into our staring contest with the haughty building when two cars pulled up at the curb on Dewey Avenue. Three other cars were already parked in the funeral home's covered driveway, including the town's only certified police car—fully radio equipped. Out of one car emerged a slender man wearing a dark suit and fedora. He walked briskly up the sidewalk, giving us a sober look through gold rimmed glasses. David pulled on my coat.

"Philip, is Dad in there?"

"Yeah, he's in there."

"Why are people going in?"

I stalled, then said, "There's been a misfortune."

"A misfortune?" David screwed up his face.

31

"You know, like what Dad said."

David looked toward the big house. "Oh," he said, his mouth actually forming a little donut **O.**

The man in the second car turned out to be our minister, Reverend Hewett. He smiled, revealing the gap between his two front teeth, and squatted down to our level. A wine-colored tie with a squiggly design on it swung out as he crouched.

"Hello, boys. On your way to school?" His breath smelled minty.

I had seen him only from the pulpit or at the front door of the church after services, so to have the Reverend actually kneeling down to talk with David and me seemed strange and unsettling. His adult-sized head was out of scale that close up, and his eyes seemed too large behind the thick lenses of rimless glasses.

He smiled and gently gripped our arms.

I nodded at his question. "We were just looking to see our dad," I said, turning my head toward the house.

He continued smiling, his smile stuck in the *on* position. "Well, I came by to see him, too. I'll let him know that you asked about him on your way to school.

How's that? He's busy right now with a very important matter."

David nodded soberly. "Yes," he said, "there's been a misfortune."

Reverend Hewett stood and looked at David curiously. "That's right, David," he said. "Well, you boys had better run along." He walked away without looking back.

When we approached the school, I ran my fingers over the chain-link fence that enclosed the schoolyard and expected to see the usual flurry of before class began, but there was no one outside. The playground around the two-story brick school house was deserted and strangely quiet. The basketball hoop nets hung limply. The swings were still. David reached for my hand when we started up the steep concrete steps. I looked at the double doors with the paned glass windows and wondered if anyone was there. The whole morning had been so eerie.

I squeezed down on the cranky handle at the top of the stairs and pulled the door open slowly, expecting, I didn't know what, but something different. The hallway was quiet, without the usual jangle of excited voices. I looked in. David hung on tight. Then suddenly there she was—Miss Bunn!

"Come in, Philip. Yes, you and…this is your brother?"

"David," I said.

"Yes, David. It's all right," she said, her voice amazingly warm. She even put her hand tenderly on my shoulder and leaned down smiling; a wave of perfume engulfed me. I could tell that her smile was orchestrated—a bit wider and her face might have cracked—but it was a smile.

There in the entryway, watching the students arrive, stood Mr. Snyder, the principal, with several teachers, and even the janitor Mr. Carson. An imposing white-haired woman was with them. Later, we were told that she was the Superintendent of Schools, Mrs. Myrtle Leach, and that it was an honor to have her visit our school.

Teachers fell on each student with comforting murmurs and escorted us to our classrooms. Off to the side, Mr. Snyder stood, a pinched half-smile tugging at his face. He really looked as if he wanted to cry. When he caught me watching him, he tried to widen his sad smile and nodded. Miss Bunn urged me along. I managed a sidelong glance toward David and gave him a quick wave. He seemed confused but managed to raise one hand and curl his fingers back at me as he was hustled off to his first-grade class.

I slid my feet down the hall—sort of ice skating—slowing when we passed what had been Mrs. Dugan's second-grade classroom. The door was closed, and a wreath of spring flowers hung on it. The bright colors seemed too cheery—like the forced smiles coming at us from all sides. Miss Bunn pushed on my shoulder, pulling my attention away from the flowers, and ushered me into her classroom. Only about half my classmates were there. That's how it was in every classroom.

Many parents kept their children home that day.

Later, Mr. Snyder took his long face to each room and used words I didn't understand to tell us about Mrs. Dugan. In my class, he said, *Mrs. Dugan, whom we all loved so much, is no longer with us. Sadly, she has departed, and it will be a long time before any of us will see her again. She was a wonderful teacher and a wonderful person. We should all think of how happy she made us feel and remember her smile always. She will be missed. For the rest of the day, we will spend time quietly at our desks in memory of Mrs. Dugan.*

At recess, I met up with Tommy Braxton and Billy Connors. We just walked around the schoolyard; no one wanted to shoot baskets or anything.

"That was dumb," Tommy said, "what Mr. Snyder said. Why didn't he say she's dead?"

"Yeah," said Billy, "we heard it on the radio. Everyone knows."

"You think so?" I asked, surprised that other kids maybe knew what being dead meant.

"Hey," said Tommy, "looka this." He began staggering around grabbing his throat and gagging, then crumbled to the ground.

He made a croaking sound and flopped his arms out and rolled his head to the side.

"He's dead," cried Billy, "he's dead. Look at me."

Billy went through his own version of dying, and we all laughed. It didn't seem funny though, not really, especially when one of the teachers stalked over and shamed us in front of everyone.

Maybe some of the younger children went home from school that day believing that Mrs. Dugan was on a trip. It was clear to me, though, that I wasn't the only kid who knew what being dead meant.

- 5 -

That day, the usual rush from the brick fortress didn't happen, there was no joyous dance of escape. School ended quietly. David and I walked home slowly along tree-lined sidewalks and back through town. You could feel it. You could see it. Wherever I looked— at women talking across their yards, men on street corners and beside parked cars, people paused on the post office steps—adults were gathered in twos and threes speaking in hushed voices. Speech was intense, heads shook in regret, mouths were drawn tight and brows were rippled. Baker City was in shock over the violence it had awakened to. When David and I passed by, some would stop talking and look at us—the children of Tiedemann, the students from her school. If our eyes met theirs, they would either squeeze out ridiculous smiles or crimp their lips and look sad. Some looked away.

I was surprised when my father showed up from work early that evening. After all, the funeral business operates twenty-four hours a day, on demand. People die when they die. When they do, someone has to go pick up the remains—don a suit coat, crank up the Cadillac funeral coach, and drive with all deliberate speed to an address where sorrowful people await. Much of the funeral business consists of waiting around for the worst to happen.

Guess I thought that my father would have to stay at the funeral home until some distant time because of the monstrous event. It wasn't only what was broadcast on the radio, or even my mother's tears, it wasn't what was said, but how it was said and the awkward behavior of the adults toward the town's children.

When my father walked through the back door near dinnertime, I turned from setting the table and studied him, expecting him to act different somehow, weakened or haggard, but he seemed the same. He always embraced my mother; this time he held her longer, but neither of them made a sound. My mother bustled about readying dinner while my father changed out of his suit. Over dinner Mom and Dad engaged in parental small talk with an air of lightness. It wasn't right. What about the murder? They were being too cheerful.

Instead of rushing outdoors when I was excused from the table, I hung back and let David scurry out unaware. I even helped my mother clear the table, a chore I usually deplored, for which I received a raised eyebrow and a smile.

I got a glass of water from the sink and hung around expecting my parents to slip into talk about Mrs. Dugan. My father lingered over a cup of coffee and intently read the front page of the paper. I shuffled past him, sipping from the glass, and snuck a look at the banner headline. The word **Murdered** leapt out at me in inch-high black type, and something tingled across my shoulders. When I could stand it no longer, I sat down again and fingered the edge of the tablecloth. My father raised his head, then went back to the newspaper.

"They had flowers on Mrs. Dugan's door at school," I said offhandedly.

My father lowered the paper and looked at me. He waited a moment, then said, "Is that right? How was it at school today, Philip? You okay?"

I shrugged. "Yeah. It was strange though, sort of—I don't know—just strange."

My mother came back to the table and sat down on the edge of a chair, a dish towel in her hand. "Did they say anything about Mrs. Dugan?"

I had their undivided attention.

"Mr. Snyder, he talked to our class about her."

When I didn't elaborate, my mother raised her eyebrows quizzically. "And?

What did he say, Philip?"

I shrugged again and moved the salt and pepper shakers around on the tablecloth. "It was kind of confusing," I said. "He talked about Mrs. Dugan being on some sort of trip. You know. That she'd be gone for a long, long time." I looked into my father's searching eyes. "It wasn't like you said, Dad, that there'd been a misfortune. Mr. Snyder never said anything like that."

My father nodded, laid the paper down, and took another swallow of coffee. He cast a look at my mother and said, "Philip...well, let me put it this way. With our family, it's different. You know a little more about such...misfortunes than most of your classmates. In our case, my job is helping people who have had tragic losses in their family. It's a regular occurrence, you might say."

"You mean when people die?"

My father moved his lips in and out, still looking at me. "Tell me what you think it means when someone dies."

I had thought about it quite a lot by that time. Anyway, I'd seen movies, and I wasn't stupid. When Zachary Scott gunned down bad guys in those crime-buster movies, it looked pretty real all right. But then again, I would see the same character all alive and well in another movie later on. So while I was pretty sure I knew what it meant to die, I didn't have it all figured out. I hedged in front of my parents and pushed the salt and pepper shakers around again. I decided to not tell them that Tommy Braxton and Billy Connors probably knew more about dying then I did.

"Well, I think it's when…I mean I'm pretty sure it's when someone quits breathing, closes their eyes and never comes back…ever."

My father was looking at me differently. "That's pretty good, Philip. You're right. Mrs. Dugan has left us and she won't be back."

"Now, Ken," my mother said "we need Philip to understand that this is table talk."

"Right. That's right." My father nodded. "Do you understand?"

"Yeah, don't say anything except to grownups."

He thought about that for a moment. "Uh, okay, yes, that's good. But for now, just keep it among the three of us. Other adults may not feel comfortable talking with you about this. Okay?" I smiled and nodded. I was in! I'd moved up another notch. I tested my new access.

"Dad, can I read about Mrs. Dugan in the paper?"

He looked down at the glaring headlines. His face twitched. It was too late to go back, and he knew it. "Okay, Son. But you have to keep our agreement. And Philip," he cautioned, "if you have questions, or if this frightens you, let me or your mother know. Okay?"

I bobbed my head and eagerly reached for the paper. At first, my father held it down—then he let it slip into my hands. I marched into the living room, dropped into my father's overstuffed armchair, and stretched to turn on the floor lamp. My eyes focused on the splash of the headline, then the small type below it. I read slowly, testing the limits of my vocabulary.

Schoolteacher Murdered

Katherine Elaine Dugan, 46-year-old teacher at Tiedemann Elementary School, living at the Pierce Apartments, 1408 Resort Street, was brutally murdered Sunday night around 10:00 p.m., according to County Coroner Arthur Woodhull. The body was discovered by three teenage Baker City boys shortly after 10:30 p.m. just off River Drive near the undeveloped area known as the Riverside Addition on the east bank of the Powder River.

According to police reports, Mrs. Dugan was assaulted with a blunt instrument; no weapon was found at the scene. County Coroner Arthur Woodhull said death resulted from wounds to the head.

No motive has yet been established, according to Chief of Police, Howard Wisdom. Robbery has been ruled out as a possible motive. Mrs. Dugan was fully clothed, and tests performed by the coroner's office indicated no criminal assault.

Miss Rachel Troutman, a resident in an apartment adjacent to that of the victim, said she heard Mrs. Dugan leave at approximately 9:00 p.m., Sunday night. Mrs. Dugan left driving her brown, 1936 Hudson sedan, which was found near the death scene.

The immediate area was cordoned off by the police and will be searched for evidence that may provide leads in the case.

Mrs. Dugan had lived in Baker City for the past nine years and taught second-grade classes at Tiedemann Elementary School during that time. She had been a resident of the Pierce Apartments since 1943. She is survived by two sons, Dwayne Dugan, 21, of La Grande, Oregon, and Floyd

Dugan, 22, of Boise, Idaho. She was divorced from her husband, Randolph Dugan, of Spokane, Washington, in 1943.

≈✻

I read the story slowly, going around some of the hard words, then I read parts of it again—about the weapon and the wounds. When I had taken in enough, I lowered the paper. My father was standing by the radio, watching me as he dipped his pipe into a blue Edgeworth tobacco pouch. He pressed his thumb into the bowl of his pipe and lit it with a kitchen match. As white smoke rose he asked, "Any questions, son?"

Reading about the gruesome death of someone you knew was like accidentally seeing your mother naked; it was too private, but you couldn't take it back. Thinking of Mrs. Dugan not being alive anymore made me feel strange. That morning, the shock of hearing the news on the radio and witnessing my parents' unprotected emotions had been exhilarating, bringing a flush of drama into our ordinary lives. It was like seeing a fire truck roar by—a blinding, momentary diversion. But the glitter had disappeared. A person I knew, a woman who had smiled at me, had been hurt so much that she was no longer a person. She wouldn't be back— ever. The words I read in the newspaper had spoken the truth so coarsely I wasn't sure that adult reality was so great after all. But it was too late to crawl back into childish innocence.

"Philip?" My father was still looking at me, holding his smoldering pipe in one hand. "Any questions?"

Questions? I looked down at the paper again. "River Drive," I said. "That's pretty close, isn't it?" I wasn't so good on street names, I just knew landmarks: The yellow house, the oak tree with the black gash in its trunk, or the old pickup with every tire squished down flat.

My father nodded. "Pretty close. A few blocks that way." He raised his arm and pointed.

In the background, I heard my mother call out the back door for David to come in. I looked out the window; the dimming dusk still seemed safe. My father followed my eyes.

"Are you worried because this happened so close to us?" he asked.

"I don't know, yeah, maybe. A little bit."

My father pushed his thumb into the bowl of the pipe again and brought the burl oval up for another light. "Hmm, well, I don't think we have to worry, but makes sense to be careful for a while. Stay close to the house. Be in before dark." He sucked the flame from another match down into the blackened bowl. "Just to be on the safe side is all. For a little while. I'm sure they'll have this solved in no time."

"Dad, why'd they do that to Mrs. Dugan? Hurt her like that?"

My father walked over and took the paper from me and folded it neatly. I remember how slack his face was and that he crimped his lips when he looked into my eyes and tapped the folded paper into the palm of his hand. "Philip, I don't know."

Just then, David rushed into the living room breathless, pink, and sweaty. Seeing him, I knew that the three years difference in our ages was now a canyon. In the face of a single traumatic event, a piece of my childhood had been left behind. Part of me liked feeling more grown up. When I looked at my little brother, though, flushed and breathing hard from a child's play, I was glad that he was still on that other side.

The murder earned top billing on the front page of the *Demo-crat-Herald*, for several days. Each evening, my father would sigh and hand me the newspaper. I would go to the overstuffed chair, sit under the floor lamp, and read the latest; mostly, it was posturing by the police and speculation by the press. My parents weren't comfortable over my absorption with the murder, but they never said anything more about it. The genie was already out of the bottle.

Two days after the body was found, police activity at the murder site was still high. After school, I had wandered over the few blocks from home to see what I could see. Several blocks—from Edgewater Avenue, down Resort Street and along the river's edge on River Drive—were cordoned off with white sawhorse barricades. Most of the town's ten-man police force were assigned to keep the curious from entering the crime scene.

On a quiet block of Edgewater, a lone police officer paced in front of a barricade with the aimlessness of a school crossing guard. When I approached, he straightened up and hooked his thumbs in the black belt that held up his pants and a holster with the butt of a revolver showing.

"Can't come in here," he said, holding up one hand, the other still hooked onto his belt, "unless you live in the neighborhood." He squinted at me, and I noticed the scraggly little mustache above his lip. "Do you?"

"No, sir," I said. "I live back over on Elm."

"Well then, you run along home, Sonny. This is a police crime scene." He spread his feet and pointed back the way I'd come.

I snuck a look beyond the public works barricades. I couldn't see anything, so I did an about-face and detoured to Freddie Patterson's Grocery where I spent the dime nestled in my pocket on an orange Popsicle. The squat little store was humming. "Fragile Freddie," so called because of him being so skinny I guess, was holding court with several ladies from the neighborhood. Not surprisingly, the topic of the day was the teacher's murder.

I slid the paper wrapper off the Popsicle and moved into a corner where I could watch Freddie Patterson deftly wielding his knife behind the meat counter, his white apron hanging loosely on his spare frame. Like an artist, he trimmed the fat from a Grade A cut of beef for Mrs. Dorsey and held it up on the palm of his hand for her inspection. She nodded and in one seamless motion he whipped a swatch of white butcher paper off the roll, folded the meat into it, ejected a wet strip of paper tape from the dispenser, slapped it into place, and handed the neat package over the meat case. It was beautiful. None of the women seemed to notice.

Mrs. Dorsey wasn't awed by Freddie Patterson's artistry like me. She dropped the package into her basket and kept right on shopping and talking. The Dorseys lived five houses down from us on Elm. Maud Dorsey and her husband, Tom—who endured unending Tommy Dorsey jokes—attended our church with their three teenagers. I had a crush on their lithe, athletic daughter,

Pearl. She could run faster and climb higher than either of her brothers and most other boys in the neighborhood. She was 16, too old for a kid like me, but when she smiled at me, I would practically burst into flame.

Mrs. Dorsey was chattering away. "It's not as if this town hasn't had its share of violence," she was saying. "What about that woman who was killed two years ago? What was her name?"

Freddie Patterson nodded. "Lilly Marks," he said, his Adam's apple bouncing.

"That's right," said another woman, older with her gray hair tied up in a bun. "Lilly Marks. She was murdered right downtown just a block off Broadway on First Street. Remember?" The woman looked around at the others in the store. "I knew her, you know." She drew herself up. "Oh yes. She belonged to my bridge club."

"What ever came of that?" asked Mrs. Dorsey.

"Nothing." The woman shook her head. "Not a thing. And such a lovely woman too—in the prime of life. And yet no one has ever been convicted of that brutal, brutal crime. It's outrageous."

I wondered if all women who died like that were *lovely* persons. My mother had said that Mrs. Dugan was "such a lovely person." And now the other woman who'd been killed was labeled the same.

"Well, you know what they say," said a woman with reddish hair and a pale face covered with hundreds of freckles. She set her shopping basket down on the counter as the others looked her way. "If you want to commit murder and get away with it, do it in Baker County."

"It's all well and good to jest about it, Nancy." The voice was that of Velma Lumpkin. She was staring at the woman with all the freckles, scowling with her pinched face, sharp nose, mass of dull brown hair, and slits for eyes. Mrs. Lumpkin lived alone in a decrepit one bedroom house over on Spring Garden Avenue. The story was that her husband went out for a quart of milk eleven years ago and never came back. Now, for Velma Lumpkin, life was simply an exercise to be endured; there was no joy in it, and she shared her bitterness with anyone who crossed her path.

She shook her finger. "I say it's time that our pathetic police force did something. Before Lilly Marks, there have been other atrocities yet unsolved."

"Oh come on now, Velma," said Freddie Patterson in his familiar twangy voice. "You make it sound like our town is a den of violence and mayhem."

"A woman's not safe on our streets. And you ought to be concerned too, Freddie," said Mrs. Lumpkin, squinting her eyes even tighter. "After all, this happened just a stone's throw from your store here. That can't be good for business."

The red haired woman named Nancy finished unloading her shopping basket onto the checkout counter and turned to confront her accuser. "I never said anything in jest, Velma. In fact, I do think we should let Chief Wisdom know that we expect action. Frankly, after what's happened, I am afraid to go out after dark."

"And me," said gray hair with bun.

"I'm not letting my children out of my sight, especially after dark," added the freckled one.

The mention of children reminded the women of my presence. Almost as one, they looked toward me, their necks on swivels. I was standing by the comic book rack with an *Archie* comic in one hand and my dripping Popsicle in the other. Freddie Patterson moved from the meat counter to the cash register, his eyes on me with every step. "Philip," he said, leaning on the counter, "unless you're buying that comic, don't get Popsicle juice all over it."

I'd been singled out. It was time to leave.

≈*

My mother was playing the piano when I entered the house. Church music—that's all she played. I slid next to her onto the piano bench; the sheet music title was *In the Garden*. She lifted her hands from the keys when she saw my orange upper lip.

"So you couldn't hang onto that dime for more than a day, huh? Stop by Freddie's?"

"Yeah." I blinked and countered with, "But, Mom, the women shopping at the store were saying that Baker County is a good place to kill people."

Typically, my mother would pass off awkward questions—and most disciplinary action—to my father. But that afternoon, with the hint of orange Popsicle still on my breath, we had a talk, she and I. We sat at the kitchen table, and she gave me a glass of milk and two homemade peanut butter cookies.

"Philip," she said, "I know that you're very curious about this tragedy.

About poor Mrs. Dugan." She closed her eyes for an instant. "We all are. And as horrible as it is, I know it seems very fascinating to you. But, Philip, I don't want you to dwell on this bad thing too much."

I chewed on the cookie and looked into my mother's eyes. "What's dwell?"

"It means giving too much attention to something. I'm concerned that you're becoming preoccupied with Mrs. Dugan's death."

I swallowed some milk. "What's preoccupied?"

She smiled. "Preoccupied means that most of your time and

thinking is being spent on this very bad thing."

Her soft blue eyes looked into mine, searching. She pushed some of my cookie crumbs into a little pile with one finger and asked me if Mrs. Dugan's death made me afraid.

I shrugged. "Afraid of what?"

"Oh, do you have bad dreams?" When I shook my head, she raised her eyebrows. "Are you afraid to be out on the street alone, like walking to school or the store?"

"Nope."

Then, my mother cocked her head and gave me a questioning look. "Really?"

"Yeah, Mom. Really. I don't have bad dreams or any stuff like that."

She smiled a gentle smile and put an open palm softly against my cheek.

That was it. She got up, cleared away my milk glass and cookie crumbs and went back to her piano.

-7-

On the fourth day after the killing, KBKR and the *Democrat-Herald* were bristling with the story of a huge reward offered by ten local businessmen. The headline screamed out that the business owners were offering a huge reward in the Dugan murder case. A full-page ad read:

$5,000.00

REWARD

For Information Leading to
the Arrest and Conviction of
the Slayer of Mrs. Katherine Dugan
the Night of May 23, 1948
The sponsors for the above are:

Leon Surrey, Tobacco Shop	G. Crabb, Cattlemen's Club
Jay Bowen, The Corral	W. Huff, Gold Dust
J. Small, Powder River Club	Ted Hickman, Gold Leaf
H. C. Hobarth, Silver Slipper	Sam Hartung, The Anthony
Geo. Worth, McGinty's	W. J. Alder, Hitching Post

In spite of this excitement, Chief Wisdom and his nine officers were turning up very few clues. Yet the murder continued to fascinate the town. Every evening after dinner, I paced around waiting for my father to finish the paper so I could pour over the latest on the investigation. Mostly, it was that the Baker City Police Department, with some help offered by the Oregon State Police, was pursuing leads that went nowhere.

School was closed on the last day of May in honor of Mrs. Dugan's funeral. The Baker Community Church sanctuary was packed; all of the pews were full, and people stood along the back wall and down the side aisles. Color was high in Reverend Hewett's face as he spoke before the largest audience of his pastorate. Among those in attendance for his solemn message were local dignitaries and businessmen, including the mayor, chief of police, district attorney, superintendent of schools, and the business owners who had put up the $5,000 reward. I think there were only two other kids from school besides me at the service; most parents kept their children away. My mother had David stay with Mrs. Dorsey. The occasion of the funeral was duly reported in the paper along with another compelling story regarding the ongoing investigation into the schoolteacher's death.

≋✷

By mid-June, Baker City residents still had a case of the jitters, partly caused by malicious gossip concerning suspects in the murder—including one unchecked rumor that a suspect had been taken secretly into custody. On top of that, nearly a dozen citizens reported to police that they had received mysterious phone calls from a gruff voiced man asking for someone who was not at that number. Police Chief Wisdom cautioned that while he took any such incidents seriously, he felt the calls may have just been a prankster trying to put an extra scare into folks.

The murder had dropped from the front page by the end of June, and most of the public nervousness had dissipated. By the

Fourth of July, it had been weeks since any account of the "Dugan Case" had been reported in the paper. Even then it had been two short paragraphs on an inside page next to a piece on local water rates. Calls from the public had gone from a flurry to a trickle. Inquiries from reporters garnered official shrugs that the police had nothing new to report.

I had given up on the story myself. With school out and summer freedom beckoning, I had the wider world to explore. My father no longer had to protect his evening paper from me; I wasn't interested in following the Dewey-Truman presidential campaign or a local controversy over sewage treatment.

That all changed the day I opened my Kool-Aid stand on our wobbly card table under the big maple tree in front of our house. I did a brisk business. I was on my fourth pitcher of purple sugar water when I suddenly had reason to close up shop. I had just pocketed twenty cents from a couple from New York driving a big yellow Chrysler with wood trim. I was giving them a toothy smile when the black Cadillac family car from Woodhull's Funeral Home pulled up in front of our house.

My father got out of the passenger side, leaned his head back in and said something to Sam Anderson who was driving. The big limousine glided away, and my father strode up the walk, his jaw set, the evening paper clamped in an armpit. He didn't say a word to me. I grabbed the nearly empty pitcher of Kool-Aid and wrestled the folded card table up the walk, left it all on the porch and went into the house. My father's voice hung in the air like the echo of a passing diesel.

"I can't believe it." His intensity swirled out on an eddy from the kitchen. "Just cannot believe it."

I stayed in the living room rather than risk being sent back outdoors. I inched up closer to the kitchen door but stayed out of sight.

"They must have good reason," said my mother, her voice even and calm.

"Read it." I heard the paper rattle. "Here, Margaret, just read it. It's all circumstantial. Jack O'Brien did not kill that woman. Damn it!"

"You don't know that. You don't know Jack O'Brien. Not really."

I heard my father pacing. "I know enough."

"My word, the police responded to a lead from Velma Lumpkin?"

My father snorted. "How about that. Of all people. She just wants that reward. That, that five thousand dollars."

My head was spinning. They were talking about Mrs. Dugan's murder. I leaned against the wall and tried to reconstruct what Jack O'Brien looked like. Since the roofing job, whenever I had been nosing around down by the river, he was never at his shack. But I still remembered how strong he looked with his shirt off and the musky smell of him as he sat beside me at dinner. Could he be the one, the killer?

My mother's voice remained level. "Or she may be a conscientious citizen.

What if this man is the murderer? Velma Lumpkin could very well be saving someone else from a similar fate as Katherine Dugan. Have you thought of that, Kenneth?"

Velma Lumpkin, the neighborhood witch. What could that woman know?

I heard my father pull out a kitchen chair and drop onto it.

"I went over to the police station, but they aren't letting anyone see Jack for the time being." There was a thud, and I guessed my father had smacked the table with his hand. "I've got to do something," he said.

"You?" My mother's voice chirped. "Ken, don't be silly. Why you?"

"Who else, Margaret? He lives alone—in that damn shack. His family is hundreds of miles away and hasn't had contact with him for years. He's unemployed. A loner who just hangs around. I guess he walks around the area where they say Mrs. Dugan was killed. So, what kind of picture does that paint for you?"

"Won't they provide him with a lawyer if he can't afford one? Don't they do that?"

"Sure they do. But Sam told me in cases like this the court usually appoints an old lawyer who hasn't practiced real law in years. A guy named Oscar Doolittle. Doolittle. And that's probably what he'll do for Jack—very little."

My mother giggled. "I'm sorry, Ken, but that is kind of funny. Besides, we certainly can't afford one thin dime to help this man."

"I know, I know." I could hear the paper rattling again. I was dying to see it.

"I can see it in your face," my mother spoke. "The set of your jaw, that look in your eyes. There's absolutely no reason for you to get involved in this. I mean, he only helped you put on a roof. That's all. Look at me, Ken. You have no obligation to that man. None."

The paper rustled again, but my father didn't respond. I strained to hear.

"This is about Warney isn't it?" my mother said.

Warney. I knew that name. My father, Warney Webster, and Steve Thompson—who would later marry my mother's only sister, Doris—grew up together in The Dalles. They were closer than brothers. I'd heard my father speak of him many times, usually when we were with my Uncle Steve. They would be sitting in the living room after Thanksgiving dinner or out in someone's backyard on a summer afternoon. Talk would turn to telling stories and laughing—until Warney's name came up.

At that point, Uncle Steve and my father would stop talking and look away. Warney hadn't lived past his nineteenth birthday. Eventually, one of them would say they sure missed old Warn. The other one would usually purse his lips and agree. They would be quiet for a bit before moving on to something else. I'd heard the whole story once. When my mother said his name, it came tumbling out again. The summer after they had graduated from high school, all three of them had jobs working in the cherry orchards. Warney began seeing the daughter of a prominent local family, a little rich girl, he called her. When they talked about it, my father and Uncle Steve lamented that they had told him he was nuts, that the girl was out of his league and playing him for a fool. But Warney was a fun-loving guy and just laughed them off. He was enjoying life, just a summer fling he'd promised.

When the pretty blonde, blue-eyed girl was found dead, strangled, Warney Webster was arrested and charged with her slaying. The town hierarchy was in an uproar, the press called for quick justice, and the city fathers promised to deliver it. No one came to Warney's defense, nor did the police follow up on a tip that a jealous boyfriend was responsible. Warney's parents were shy, unsophisticated people who, in their confused and terrified state, didn't know what to do. They fumbled about desperately seeking legal help, but nine days after being arrested, Warney Webster hanged himself in his jail cell.

"You can't erase what happened, Ken," my mother said. "You can't make up for Warney by getting involved in this."

My father didn't respond at first. There was a span of dead air before he said, "We waited around sucking our thumbs. All the while Warney was terrified, but we thought everything would be all right." A kitchen chair scrapped back and my father said, "I'm calling John Hewett."

"John? What on earth for? You want John to visit Jack?"

My father was exasperated. "No, no. I just remembered that that attorney, Haskin MacHall, goes to our church." As I was soon to learn, Haskin MacHall was not just an attorney, he was *the* attorney in Baker City, on a shelf by himself.

My father stormed out of the kitchen to the telephone stand in our living room. I was trapped. Catching sight of me out of the corner of his eye, he whirled to find me plastered up against the wall. He stopped and squinted at me, his oval face uncharacteristically roped in anger.

"Eavesdropping are we, Philip?"

My face burned, and I shrugged, smiling weakly. Without another word he went to the phone, found the number, and dialed. He looked back over at me, where I stood stark still—feeling like a cowering sneak—then he turned back to the phone.

"John." My father's voice erupted into the mouthpiece. "Ken Wade. Have you seen today's paper, or listened to the radio? That's okay. Anyway, they've arrested a man named Jack O'Brien? Huh? For the murder of Katherine Dugan, the teacher. Yes. Listen, I know Jack O'Brien. He did some work for me. Anyway…yes, I had him help me put a new roof on our house. Anyway, John, there's no way Jack did this thing."

My father listened and nodded, then shook his head.

"No, I don't believe it. Read the paper. It's all circumstantial."

More listening, this time with his jaw muscles flexing.

"Let's not get into that now. Look, John, the man needs a lawyer. They want to foist him off on a court appointed geezer because Jack can't afford his own lawyer. Anyway, I was thinking of Haskin MacHall. Maybe you could arrange a meeting with him? Well, I would, but I don't know him personally. I thought maybe you could open the door for me."

I was quiet as dew listening to my father angle for a favor. Reverend Hewett must have had a lengthy response because my father just listened for a bit. He sat on the arm of the sofa and looked at a spot on the wall.

"I know, John, but I'm the new guy in town. You know the man, and you are his pastor. That's more leverage than I have. All I want to do is talk with MacHall. This could get messy. It's critical that Jack O'Brien gets a good lawyer. I know, John, listen…I know, but even if he is guilty, it has to be clean. No dirty tricks and no quick conviction to help the police and the district attorney look good.

"So, will you do it? All I want is a brief meeting and a chance to lay out some facts." My father chewed on his lip. "Good. We need to move fast. See if he'll meet with me this evening. His office, maybe the parsonage. I'll go wherever it'll work. It would be good if you could be there too. Huh? Maybe you're right, the parsonage is not a good idea. Besides, I don't have a car. How about coming to my house? Right. Let me know."

My father held the phone in his hand for a moment then dropped it into the cradle. I was still up against the wall next to the kitchen door, not sure if I should bolt through the door and run away to Montana or take my medicine. I decided to give it my best shot.

"Look, Dad," I blurted, "I was just…"

He pushed a hand at me and shook his head. "Never mind, Philip. It's okay." He walked past me and a moment later came back and handed me the paper. "I know you want to read this."

At first, it was impossible for me to move or to start breathing normally. But my curiosity soon pushed all of that away, and I was in the armchair unfolding the paper. There it was, Tuesday, July 13, big and black:

Suspect Arrested in Dugan Slaying

Baker City Police Chief, Howard Wisdom, said today that Jack O'Brien, 32, of this city, has been arrested as a suspect in the May 23 slaying of Katherine Elaine Dugan, a second-grade schoolteacher at Tiedemann Elementary School and nine-year Baker City resident. O'Brien, originally from Huntington, has been a resident of Baker City since 1946, following his discharge from the U.S. Army. The suspect has been living in a one-room building only a few blocks from the site of the Dugan slaying.

The arrest was made by Baker City Police following a tip from Mrs. Velma Lumpkin, 47, of 609 Spring Garden Avenue. Mrs. Lumpkin, who said she regularly exercises her dog between her home and the empty lots adjacent to the murder site on River Drive, told police that she had seen O'Brien in the vicinity on several occasions and became suspicious because he was always alone and his demeanor at times seemed threatening.

The Dugan case, though unsolved, has remained open and active, according to the police, and every lead is followed up. A search warrant was obtained, and police entered O'Brien's residence. In light of evidence found there, a warrant for O'Brien's arrest was issued, and he was brought into custody.

The *Democrat-Herald* has learned that the most crucial evidence leading to an arrest was the presence of bloody rags in O'Brien's residence. Tests on the rags found the blood samples to be type O-positive, later confirmed as the blood type of Katherine Elaine Dugan. O-positive is the most common blood type among the general population, including that of the suspect. O'Brien also had a scar from a recent wound on his right hand.

Also found at the O'Brien residence were a number of tools and other heavy implements which are being examined as possible murder weapons.

When Baker County District Attorney, T. C. Wingate, was queried, he acknowledged that a preliminary hearing to establish probable cause that O'Brien may have committed the murder will be set shortly.

≕✿

Reverend Hewett called back within half an hour to say Haskin MacHall had agreed to meet at our house that evening. My father listened, and his jaw muscles begin to flex. I knew something wasn't right. At one point he said, "Okay, okay, if that's the way is has to be," and jammed the receiver down. The attorney had agreed to come but only on the condition that some of the church leadership be asked sit in. In addition to MacHall's prominence in the community, he was also chairman of the church board.

My father stood for a long moment with his hand still on the downed receiver, then he cursed and drove his fist into the palm of his hand. I had a crawly feeling in my stomach seeing my father's anger. He stomped into the kitchen, drew a glass of water at the sink, and began to rant about Jack O'Brien and meddle-some do-gooders getting in the way. My father's anger had always been the low rumbling kind, quiet and firm. To see him thrashing around the kitchen, gulping water, and literally roaring both frightened and intrigued me.

When the glass shattered in the sink, I couldn't tell if my father had smashed it or if it had slipped from his hand. My mother took my father's hands in hers and examined them for cuts before picking the glass fragments out of the sink and dropping them in the waste can under the sink. He stood quietly by and watched stone-faced until she turned to him and asked if he was finished. He nodded.

≈✿

That evening, I hung around by the front door waiting for the men to arrive. Reverend Hewett arrived early. He flashed a fake smile at me.

"Philip, boy. How you doing?"

"Fine."

"Good, good."

He patted me on the shoulder and slipped by in one stride to meet my father coming the other way. My father had put on a fresh dress shirt and tie. The two men mumbled greetings, and Reverend Hewett launched right into a rapid-fire defense.

"Ken, I know you didn't want it this way. Honestly, at first Haskin didn't see this having any bearing on the church."

"I never said it did, John. In fact, it doesn't."

"I know, and I told him you just wanted to talk to him about this man O'Brien. I did really. But he suddenly reversed himself. Since Katherine Dugan was a member of the church, he thinks maybe there is a connection that should be considered."

My father was shaking his head, his lips crimped. "For the love of Mike. I only want the man to consider representing Jack or at least help get him decent counsel."

Reverend Hewett shrugged. "I know."

"Not engage in a religious debate."

"Oh, I don't think it will come to that. I'm sure not."

With each twisted clink of our doorbell, I admitted them one by one. Thomas Dorsey, chairman of the elders, arrived with a toothpick in his mouth. He smiled and patted me in passing. The one I knew best, Wendell Grier, the choir director, a tall, colorless man, with wiry steel wool black hair, didn't give me a sideways glance. Haskin MacHall and Dr. Bryant Givler, a local physician and vice chair of the board, arrived together.

MacHall moved as if he had nothing to prove to anyone. He was balding and red-faced, his skin the kind that brightens in the sun and stays that way. In contrast, Dr. Givler was young, trim, and filled with vigor. I liked him.

The male voices vibrated against the ceiling and back down. My father stood among them and greeted each man with funereal regret. This wasn't going the way he wanted. My mother and David brought in coffee and cookies, and at that moment, my father sent me from the room. Humiliated, I walked past the quiet faces and shut the kitchen door. David was already outside the back door playing cars in the dirt. No children's games for me. I plastered an ear up against the door, but I could hear only the tantalizing edge of words.

When it was over, the men's voices pooled into an exiting hum. Heavy feet shuffled onto the front porch, and cars started up. I opened the kitchen door and found John Hewett standing with his hands at his sides and my father saying goodbye to Tom Dorsey. He closed the door, rubbed open palms over his face and gave a grunting sound, drawing a laugh from Reverend Hewett.

"What'd I tell you, John?" My father folded his arms across his chest and scrunched up his shoulders. "The Tower of Babel."

John Hewett's cherub cheeks were rosy in the aftermath. "Oh, it wasn't that bad," he said. "All in all, it was a good exercise I think. Got everyone's opinions out in the open. Besides, Haskin didn't turn you down."

"Didn't say yes, either."

"I think he just wanted to test the waters. You know, how would people take it if he did end up representing Jack O'Brien? This was a dry run."

"Dry run? We can't waste time. Jack needs help right now. This isn't something you decide by some dang committee." My father hugged himself and stared at the floor. "I keep thinking of him locked up. Imagine if it was you, John. Think on that. Being locked up. The whole town thinking you killed someone. Ready to string you up. Imagine how you'd feel."

Reverend Hewett blinked, and his face reddened even more. "I can't."

My father shook his head. "Exactly. So this…this gathering of the pious is irrelevant. Useless."

"Guess I can ask you the same question, Ken. Can't I?"

"Do I know how it would feel, locked in a cell, no hope?" My father's eyes were sad. "I do, John. Sorry to say, I do. I've seen this kind of hysteria before." He paused and inhaled. "It ended horribly, believe me."

He put a hand on John Hewett's shoulder and all but ushered the bewildered man out the door. It was clear that my father had had enough of justice by committee.

He closed the door, sighed a ragged breath, and turned to find my mother standing in the kitchen doorway studying him, one hand in the patch pocket of her apron. My mother's posture was erect, questioning. Facing empty cups and cookie crumbs, my parents broke from their frozen stance, and we cleaned up without comment. With the last saucer stored, my father dropped onto a kitchen chair and stared at the floor.

David came in carrying a little red truck, smudges of dirt on his face. The screen door slapped closed behind him. He looked around and wanted to know what was wrong. My mother cooed over him and scooted him off for a bath.

With David tucked in, my mother returned to the kitchen and joined us at the table. My father still sat quietly leaning on his elbows.

"All right, Ken. We dutifully sat out here in the kitchen, quiet as mice. Now what happened? Tell us."

My father sat up and let out a rolling sigh. "All I wanted…it was simple, Margaret, all I wanted was to meet with Haskin MacHall. That's it. Talk with him alone—just him and me—about his looking into Jack's situation. Get him to go see Jack, face to face, and then maybe take on his case for no fee. Instead," he raised his hands and pawed the air, "I got this…this, I don't know what to call it. A pack of the righteous sitting around clucking like pompous twits."

"Ken, what happened?"

My father raised his eyebrows and stared at nothing. "Should've called MacHall direct, not got John in on it. I goofed. Doesn't have a thing to do with the church. Not really." He blinked. "It ended up being a pointless bull session. An asinine debate about the church's position in the matter." He shook his head. "Can you believe it? I swear, this same bunch couldn't decide what color to paint a white church. The choir director was even in on it, for god's sake."

"Ken," my mother admonished.

Waving her off, he stood and paced slowly around the table. "To begin with," he said, "when I told them that I know Jack O'Brien and didn't think he was guilty. There was dead silence. And that all I had wanted was a one-on-one with Haskin, not a church meeting." My father pushed his glasses up and rubbed his eyes with his knuckles, chuckling. "Boy, if you ever want to get a rise out of someone, just imply that they aren't needed. Once I hinted they weren't relevant, everyone had an opinion. 'We must consider the reputation of the church. What business did we have meddling in police business? Christian compassion. How would it look if we sided with the man who is later proven to be the killer of one of our flock?'"

"What if that's true?" my mother asked.

"Margaret, so what if Katherine Dugan sang in the choir? She probably shopped at J. C. Penney, too. Maybe Haskin MacHall bought a suit there. Does that mean we should have had the store manager in on our meeting?" He leaned against outstretched arms on the kitchen counter and lowered his head.

My mother laughed.

"Well it's that ridiculous. I wanted an attorney, who just happens to be a member of my church. That's all, for crying out loud. The church is not involved.

"MacHall didn't say a word during all of this. Just nibbled on cookies and looked bored. When the cookies were gone, he looked at his watch and said that he'd think about it."

"Well, that's something anyway," said my mother.

My father let out a grunt. "Just a game. We have coffee and cookies and an innocent man sits in jail."

"You can't make this personal, Ken. It's...well, it's just something that happened. You aren't responsible."

"Of course it's personal. I know the man and he's alone, totally alone."

My mother let that pass and began folding her apron. She looked at me and said, "Philip, this is table talk, you understand?"

I nodded.

"Okay. Now off to bed."

Long after I pulled the covers up under my chin, I could hear the muffled sounds of my parents' voices coming from the kitchen—mainly the sound of my father venting his frustration. They were still at it when I finally drifted off.

≈✹

With the alleged murderer of Katherine Dugan in jail, the town was alive with relief and primed for justice. Reports on KBKR and stories in the *Democrat-Herald* and the weekly *Record-Courier* were continual. Every detail of the investigation and every known fact about Jack O'Brien were told again and again. In the face of all the fervor, my father went to the jail every day insisting that he be allowed to see O'Brien because he was the only close contact the man had. In the end, he was granted visitation, twenty minutes. My father was disturbed by Jack O'Brien's haggard appearance and his intense response to the visit, the welling of tears and the seizure of my father's hand that had to be gently pulled away. O'Brien had no idea that anyone cared. Their visit was hushed and brief. My father came away worked up and even more convinced of the man's innocence.

After dinner that same day, my mother and I sat at the kitchen table and listened intently as my father told us the whole story. The blood-stained rags were Jack O'Brien's all right, but he claimed that they were bloodied when he was replacing a broken window in the shack. He had cut his hand—that was how he got the scar. The tools the police found were just ordinary tools—a hammer, a pry bar, an old hand saw, pliers and screw drivers—tools any man would have. O'Brien said, sure, he walked that part of town a lot. Resort Street and River Drive were streets he regularly used. And yeah, he remembered seeing Mrs. Lumpkin and her dog, but he left people alone and never struck up casual conversations. Jack O'Brien was adamant that he had never known or encountered Katherine Dugan. He had seen her picture in the paper, and she was not a person he recognized. My father promised to visit Jack O'Brien as often as they would let him.

By midweek, my father hadn't heard from the attorney, Haskin MacHall, and with each passing day he grew more impatient. That wasn't the only dead-end. Jack O'Brien had given my father his brother's phone number in California, but when he reached Dennis O'Brien in Fresno, the older sibling wanted nothing to do with Jack or his problems. The news account of the murder and Jack's arrest had made their local paper, but the brother said that his family had no intention of becoming involved. Even when my father expressed his own belief in Jack's innocence, the response was, *not interested and don't call again.*

≥✣

My father stewed and waited to hear from the attorney; waited and stewed. He wanted to break things loose for Jack O'Brien, but he couldn't do it by his own efforts or by his own will. The tension began building in my father right after the meeting with the men from the church. He became a stranger in our house. There were outbursts, awkward spits of anger that left all of us mystified and demoralized. My father made more visits to see Jack O'Brien only to return more angry and frustrated about what to do for the man. I would find him sitting in the dark, staring at nothing, willing only to grunt at my questions.

Some nights after dinner he would say he had to go back to work and not come home until late. One night I was awakened by the sound of him returning after one such outing. I wandered into the living room and found him sitting in the dark smoking his pipe. The light from the hall fell on him. He looked up at me, his face flushed, and smiled, but it was not the smile I was used to.

"Philip," he said. His skin looked moist, and his eyelids were lazy. "How you doing, son?"

"Okay."

He puffed on his pipe and laid his head back on one of Mom's doilies. "Been a long day," he said.

When he spoke there was a sour earthy smell. There'd never been any alcohol in our house, but I knew that that was the odor on my father's breath. He patted me on the arm and told me to get on back to bed. I laid in the dark listening until he shuffled into the bathroom and peed and burped and mumbled something before tiptoeing into a darkened bedroom. During the night when I got up to go to the bathroom, I heard snoring and wondered what my mother was thinking of his strange behavior. But during those days she was silent. If she was displeased with my father's lapses, she kept it to herself. If she ever took him to task for the drinking, it was done in private, away from her sons' ears.

≈✦

Every Thursday evening, my mother played piano for choir practice. Since we still didn't have our own car, Wendell Grier, the choir director, gave her a ride in his 1939 Chevrolet coupe. When my father was on evening duty at Woodhull's, David and I had to go to choir practice with my mother. It was a tight fit in that musty coupe with me in the middle on the scratchy mohair bench seat, my chin at elbow level. I caught more than one knock in the chin whenever Wendell Grier turned the wheel, and I had to try and keep my knees out of the way every time he used the floor shift. David would lie on the shelf up behind the seat. Grier soon tired of that arrangement, and for the rest of the time, David and I rode in the trunk with the lid propped open by one spindly, mechanical arm. So there we rode, the two of us, looking backward, often staring into the faces of people following closely in another car. But that was okay. I didn't like sitting next to Mr. Grier, anyway, dodging his elbow and the gear shift. Besides, he always had bad breath.

The Thursday after the men's meeting at our house, my father was on duty, so David and I had to go to choir practice. Wendell

Grier's trunk was full of bags of something for his yard so we had to ride up front again. We all squeezed in, Grier ground the starter, and the Chevy lurched off down Elm Street.

We had bounced along for a couple of blocks when he said offhandily, "By the way, Margaret, how is Ken taking all of this...you know, this thing with that fellow?"

"You mean Jack O'Brien?"

Grier's eyes widened, and he looked down at me as if my mother had said *sex* out loud. "Well, yes. I assume he's given up any idea about getting involved in that sordid business. Hasn't he?"

I felt my mother's body tense. "No. Ken is convinced the man is innocent. He wants to help him."

Grier pulled to a stop at Main and Bridge streets and looked both ways. "Don't you think it's foolish for Ken to take such a... well, a personal interest? What does he know of this fellow, really?" He accelerated, turning right onto Main Street.

My mother looked straight ahead. "When someone feels they're right, it is *personal*."

"Yes, but the police have a clear-cut case." Grier looked over my head at my mother. "It's almost certain that the guy'll..." He looked down at me again. "Well, that he'll be convicted."

My mother rested her hand on my leg and squeezed my thigh so hard I yelped. "Sorry, dear," she said. "Well, Wendell, it seems Mr. O'Brien is being held on largely circumstantial evidence. A long way from any conviction, I should think." She spoke my father's words as if they were her own, almost as if she believed what she was saying.

Wendell Grier stripped a gear and said, "The evidence may be circumstantial, but there's a stack of it, and the talk everywhere is that O'Brien is...is the one. I think Ken is wasting his time, no matter his noble intent."

Then my mother did the unpardonable: She rolled her prized sheet music into a tube and squeezed it. "I'm sure Ken will do whatever his conscience and principles dictate, regardless of town gossip." My neck was on a swivel, following the exchange.

When Wendell Grier curbed the coupe in front of the church, my mother had her door open and was out of the car before the choir director had set the hand brake. "Come on, boys," she hastened. We left Mr. Grier looking after us, bewildered.

Two hours later, after the piano was silenced and song sheets were stored—and except for a couple of stripped gears—we rode home in silence. Grier quietly thanked my mother, and she quietly thanked him as he tried, without success, to give us boys a playful goodbye.

That Sunday, my father attended church for the first time in weeks. The Dorseys crowded us into their Ford, kids sitting on laps and on the floor board, but nothing was said about "that matter" on the drive to and from the church. Maud Dorsey and my mother kept the conversation upbeat, about anything other than Jack O'Brien. To my father's bitter disappointment, Haskin MacHall was out of town, so he wasn't able to talk with him after church as he'd planned. His fixation on getting Jack a lawyer had to be postponed again. The early fervor over capturing the animal that had killed Mrs. Dugan had changed to a cold certainty that Jack O'Brien would stand trial and be sentenced to death. My father was becoming more sullen and less responsive to the family, and his face was a permanent knot of concentration. The smile I knew was absent. He more often sat in his chair under the floor lamp, writing in his notebook. One time I saw him with an old photo album looking at one picture for a long time, holding it up beneath the lamp to see it more clearly. I was pretty sure it was a picture of Warney Webster.

Then on Monday, our home was invaded.

My Grandma Wade had long told my father that she intended to visit us in Baker City, but she didn't know for sure when it would be. She was supervisor of nursing for the Oregon State Tuberculosis Hospital & Sanitarium in The Dalles. She worked long hours so her promise to visit was never taken seriously. But on Monday morning, around 10 o'clock, my mother answered the phone to find Hannah Wade on the other end of the line. She was in town at the bus depot. She had just arrived and intended to stay for several days. Twenty minutes later the Thirteen Taxi pulled up in front of our house. My mother and we boys stood out on the front porch watching the driver lug two heavy suitcases up the walk as Grandma Wade preceded him waving vigorously to her surprised hosts.

Her daughter-in-law met her with a hug. "Hannah, how good to see you—and such a surprise. Ken didn't mention that you were going to visit." My mother's tight smile went unnoticed.

"I didn't tell him. Just decided to come last night. I had an opening at work and took it." She pinched David's cheek. He pulled back, rubbing the offended spot. Grandma Wade was nearly sixty then. She was a tall woman who carried herself erectly, peering out aloofly at people through round, steel-rimmed glasses. She had a prominent, angular nose and silver-gray hair pulled back and held in place with combs. Her voice was nasal, but she used it with authority. No one ignored my grandmother.

She paid the cab driver and said, "Well, let's get settled in shall we?" And just that quickly, Grandma Wade was the woman of the house. Within a few minutes, it had all been decided. I would sleep on the couch in the living room, David would sleep with our parents, and Grandmother would take our room.

While Grandma Wade unpacked, my mother quietly called her husband at work to give him the "good" news. Her words were very focused and insistent. I wondered if the hovering cloud of

Jack O'Brien would be put under wraps, if my father would mask his anger, or if he even cared to in spite of his mother's visit.

After my mother had finished speaking to my father, Grandma Wade emerged, looked about imperiously, and declared that the bus trip had been tiring, and she was going to take a nap. With that, David and I watched her stride back into our bedroom and close the door. We were exiled. After a moment of stunned silence, our mother came out of her bewilderment and shooed us outside so that our sudden guest could have quiet.

We scuffed around the yard. David went up on the front porch and peeked in the window. He came back and said, "I don't want to sleep with Mommy and Daddy."

"You have to," I said.

"Daddy snores and makes funny noises."

I wondered which bed Grandma Wade was sleeping in. Was it mine? Would my pillow smell different? "Forget it," I said. "Let's go to the tunnel."

David smiled and hopped a couple of times. He liked exploring the tunnel. We scrambled up the hillside and started into the cool, dusty passage only to be startled by a muffled voice coming at us out of the dark.

"Hey, what you two doin'?" It was Jimmy Purdue. He was a year ahead of me in school and lived in the neighborhood over on Walnut Street. He was big for his age, buck-toothed and always getting into some kind of trouble. Much of his troublesome nature was mimicked after two older bothers who were known around town for being belligerent toughs. Jimmy idolized their every move; it didn't look good on him.

"We're gonna crawl through," I answered. "What are you doin'?"

"Ah, just hanging around. Want a cigarette?" He held out a package of Lucky Strikes. I could smell the smoke and see the burning cigarette in his other hand.

"Nah," I said.

"What's the matter? Chicken?"

"No. I just don't want to, that's all."

He wiggled the cigarette pack under my nose and clucked like a chicken. I pushed his hand away. "Chicken. Chicken. Hey, your old man hired that killer, didn't he? He put on that shitty roof of yours, didn't he?"

"So what? And besides, he isn't a killer."

"Yeah, we know your old man is in cahoots with that murderer, that Jack O'Brien creep. The cops say he killed the teacher, that Miz Dugan, and my dad and my brothers know he done it, too. He's gonna get the chair for sure."

I ran from the taunts and caught up to David with Jimmy Purdue still shouting after me. His words echoed along the tunnel walls but were soon muffled and indiscernible.

By this point, David and I had to lean over because the tunnel ceiling was getting lower with each step. All I heard now was the quiet sloughing of our feet in the dust and the sound of our own breathing. I clunked my head against a low beam and sat down to rub the pain out. David came back and sat down beside me.

"What'd that kid mean? Is that man gonna have to sit in the corner like at school?"

"What do you mean?" I rubbed my head some more.

"He said he'd have to sit in a chair for being bad to my teacher. Didn't he?"

"No, not like that. It's something different, another kind of chair," I said like I knew. I could only imagine that the chair Jimmy Purdue spoke of was some kind of horrible punishment.

David merely said, "Oh," then hunched over a bit and trotted off ahead of me, his silhouette moving like a bobbing dwarf.

We came out of the tunnel onto a ledge in bright heat and sat blinking. We looked down at an old rock quarry below. A rusty steel cable hung down from somewhere above us. We decided to use it to climb down. It didn't look too hard. I inched out and reached for the cable, but before I could get a firm grip on it, the rocky edge crumbled. I was going over. Then I felt David's little hand grab the back of my belt. He pulled and pulled, and I backpedaled frantically with both feet scooting back onto the ledge. David held onto my belt for a long time. After waiting for our hearts to quit hammering, we inched down the cliff using the cable.

Once we were at the bottom, I stood and looked up and felt a tingle. It would have been a long fall. Then, we scrambled across the rocky vacant lot at the base of the cliff and walked back on Spring Garden Avenue where we came up on Velma Lumpkin's house. An old Chevrolet sat in the gravel drive amid engulfing weeds. I wondered if that wreck of a car was all that remained of her husband who'd gone for the milk. Out of curiosity, I stopped and looked into the yard, past the picket fence with its missing teeth to the brown patches of weeds where a lawn should have been and at the bedraggled building, its white paint chalky and peeling.

David stood beside me. "Why you stoppin'?"

"That Mrs. Lumpkin, she lives here," I said. "She told the police to arrest Jack O'Brien."

My little brother's face puckered. "She's bad, isn't she?"

"What you kids doing there?" The voice rose from behind us. Cold needles grabbed the back of my neck, and I spun around to see Velma Lumpkin striding up the street with both arms wrapped around a grocery sack. She was wearing a formless, green house dress, and her hair was wild.

"Well! Just what are you up to—no good I suspect." She was yelling. David stayed behind me and grabbed onto my belt.

"Nothing," I said. "We aren't doing anything."

"I don't believe you. I ought to call the police."

My eyes watered, and my stomach rolled. What if she did call the police? Could they arrest us for just looking into somebody's yard? I thought maybe they could. Maybe I would end up in the same jail cell as Jack O'Brien.

On an impulse I blurted, "You shouldn't have put the police onto Jack O'Brien! He didn't hurt anyone."

"So that's it," Velma Lumpkin snorted. "I know you. Both of you. You're them Wade kids. Your father's siding with that murderer. Well, they've got him now." She tossed her head back and stomped past us, a stalk of celery waving from her shopping bag. She turned at the driveway. "Now get on out of here." She waved her arm. "And don't let me see you around here again."

"You're bad!" David hollered.

Velma Lumpkin turned without responding and marched off, back into her own world behind a slammed door. David and I ran the rest of the away down Spring Garden, stopping only to catch our breath before crossing Highway 30. I looked toward town, half expecting to hear a police siren.

-10-

Any dread of Velma Lumpkin was wiped away by the sight of a big car parked in front of our house. We circled it on tip toe and peered into an open side window. It was a Packard—shiny, light blue, four door. *Super 8* read a chrome plate. I loved looking at cars because we didn't have one. If a car could be arrogant, that one was. Brilliant white sidewall tires, leather upholstery, and an upright chrome grill with its nose in the air. Then it came to me: It had to be Haskin MacHall's. The attorney must have come to visit my father about Jack O'Brien. At last.

David and I crashed through the back door, the screen door doing a double-slam, and were immediately shushed by our mother. She and Grandma Wade were sitting at the kitchen table, each with a cup of tea. The door to the living room was closed.

"There's a big car outside," David said all breathless.

"Quiet now, boys," my mother said, looking at us with a frown, examining the tunnel dirt on our clothes. "Your father has a guest. Wash up in the sink."

"It's that Mr. MacHall, isn't it?" I asked, watching brown water circle down the drain.

"Yes it is," she said quietly. I looked over my shoulder, and her eyes bore straight into mine.

I sidled over to the closed door and listened but heard nothing. I felt a twinge like I always did when adults around me whispered or stepped away so I couldn't hear.

"Is it about Jack O'Brien?"

"Perhaps."

My grandmother's eyes widened. "My word, Margaret. Don't tell me these children know about that—" She paused, searching for the word. "That...matter."

My mother tilted her head and shrugged. "This is a small town, Hannah, and it was a teacher from the boys' school after all."

"Well, yes, but just think what this may..."

"Ken and I—and the boys—are handling this our own way." My mother's voice was soft but weighted. She poured more tea and calmly met my grandmother's look of incredulity.

David and I were having ginger snaps and milk when my father opened the kitchen door. He stood in the doorway, hands shoved into his pockets, his dark blue tie and shirt collar loosened at the neck. He smiled. It was the first smile I'd seen on his face in so long it almost looked fake. Grandma Wade was looking at him, my mother was looking at him—we were all looking at him.

"Well?" the two women said in unison.

"I'll be damned," my father said ignoring their raised eyebrows. "He's going to do it. Gonna go see Jack, maybe even represent him. I can't believe it."

My father was energized again. Vigor replaced the gloom I'd seen for days and days. I looked for my mother's reaction, expecting apprehension. Instead I found no expression at all, nothing but benign composure. Grandma Wade set her teacup down and looked at her son.

"Kenneth," she said, her tone cool. My father's smile switched off. "I've learned just enough to form an opinion," she said to him. "This awful thing with this…this O'Brien person is something you had best drop. You have your children and your wife to think of—not to mention your reputation. I can see it from an objective point of view. Maybe you can't." She folded her napkin neatly and looked at her only child. "It is a sordid business and something you should not be involved with."

My father stood unmoving as his mother spoke, his head tipped down, his eyes hooded. When she had finished, he looked up directly into her eyes.

"Mother," he said, "come with me."

Her head moved back almost imperceptibly as she met his gaze. "And what for?"

"We'll talk, just come." He stepped to the kitchen doorway and waited.

For a long moment nothing happened as mother and son held each other's gaze. But in the end, Grandma Wade set aside her napkin with great dignity, rose from her chair, and preceded her son into the living room. My father closed the door, and the kitchen was sealed in a vacuum yet again—airless and still. The humming of the refrigerator was the only sound until David whispered, "Mom, can I have another cookie?" My mother laughed, and we breathed again.

I never learned what my father said to Grandma Wade, but for the rest of her stay with us, she never again mentioned Jack O'Brien. She was mostly cheerful and held her opinion-giving in check—mostly.

The next day, in the middle of a cloudless July morning, Haskin MacHall visited Jack O'Brien in jail and, after hearing his story, agreed to represent him. The fee was one dollar, a crinkled bill which was proudly advanced by my father. Word of MacHall's visit with O'Brien quickly spread. Just as quickly, the story appeared in the *Democrat-Herald*, and at KBKR the announcer, Herb Gaskill, led his news broadcast with the report of MacHall's involvement in the murder case. Because of the attorney's standing, his sudden involvement may have slowed what my father called the gallows juggernaut and given some people reason to reconsider their rush to judgement.

Prior to MacHall entering the case, public opinion was certain that the police had the murderer in custody and that it was only a matter of time before he would be executed. If a person of Haskin MacHall's stature was willing to represent an unpopular client then doubt was no longer ruled out. What if the police didn't have the real killer after all? In any case, it gave Jack O'Brien his first hope of fair treatment.

Even in a town of only 9,425 residents, my father was an unknown newcomer. We Wades were average citizens, my folks struggling to get by. Up until the time Haskin MacHall stepped in, only a handful of people knew that Jack O'Brien had anyone acting as his defender. MacHall's entrance changed that. Because of the renewed interest in the case, my father's advocacy of Jack O'Brien was reported as part of the revived story. Overnight, we were no longer human wallpaper, and my father became a magnet for those most angry and fearful. Anonymous voices uttered hostilities over the phone. Crude letters arrived unsigned. One set of neighbors suddenly wouldn't let their kids play with David and me.

I answered one of those calls a couple of days after the newspaper story.

My mother and Grandma Wade had walked to Patterson's Grocery so I was alone in the house. "This the Wade place?" The male voice was low and breathy. When I said yes, the man asked, "Your dad home, kid?" He wasn't. "Well, you listen, then." The person inhaled raggedly. "You tell him he's a scum-sucking son of a bitch. You got that, kid?" I couldn't speak. "Tell him to stay the fuck out of this O'Brien thing. That asshole is guilty, and he's gonna sizzle for what he's done." The voice stopped and the breaths came faster. "You tell him that. He's been warned."

I was still shaky when I intercepted my father on the bridge that day. He listened quietly as I repeated what the voice on the phone had said. He put his arm across my shoulders, and for awhile we both looked down into the river's murky current. Afterward, we walked home, and he told my mother about the call. She looked at me, back at my father, and massaged her hands for a few moments before she said, "No." From that day on, until things changed, I was not allowed to answer the phone.

A few members of our church openly disagreed with my father, too. Others censured with their silence. It was like he had committed a horrible sin. One Sunday after services, we were waiting out in front of the church for my mother when Mr. Ira Twiggle, a local public accountant, marched up to my father with his wife in tow. He was short, thin, and very bald. He had slender fingers and map-like blue veins on the backs of his hands. He stood turning the brim of his hat and squinted up at my father.

"Mr. Wade," he said.

"Mr. Twiggle," my father smiled politely and nodded to his wife, who stood with her hands clasped in front of her significant stomach. "Mrs. Twiggle." She tilted her head back a trifle, elevating her severe posture even more. They were an odd couple—the twig and the oak.

Ira Twiggle cleared his throat, still turning the hat. "Mrs. Dugan was a lovely person," he said, his voice wavering on the edge of nervousness.

There it was again. Murdered women were all lovely persons. I was sure that Mrs. Twiggle would escape that label.

My father nodded. "Yes, yes she was."

"Yes...well that's easy enough to say, but we've known her... well, we knew her for many years. She was truly an instrument of the Lord through her voice and her teaching."

My father nodded benignly. "Of course you're right," he said. "We did know her for only a short while. But in that time, her goodness was evident. My wife saw this with the choir."

Ira Twiggle blinked nervously through rimless, bifocals. "Well then," he said, "how can you do it? How can you defend her murderer?"

My father's smile faded. "Why shouldn't I stand by someone I feel is wrongly accused?"

Still turning his hat, the man started when he heard his wife's grunt of admonition. "Wrongly accused? The man is an animal. An abomination. Depraved. Evil. The police have him dead to rights. The evidence is clear. They are the righteous purveyors of the Lord's vengeance. Leave his judgment to them." He stepped back, his eyes blinking. "You stay out of it."

It was one of the few times I ever saw my father completely baffled. He looked over at Irene Twiggle then back at her husband.

"Good heavens, man," my father said, "where's your compassion? Even the condemned have the right to a fair trial."

"My compassion?" Twiggle looked back at his wife. "Our compassion? It is for and with our lost sister. One of our number. If you can't see that, Mr. Wade, maybe you and your family...well, maybe you just don't belong here. Frankly, your position is disgraceful." He straightened his diminutive self as tall as heredity would allow and sniffed. "We felt it our duty to speak out."

With that said, Ira Twiggle latched onto his wife's arm and guided her bulk down the sidewalk, her mincing steps painful to watch as fleshy, swollen feet bulged from dainty dress shoes. My father watched after them. Then he walked across the street where the Dorseys waited to drive us home and sent them on their way. We walked home that Sunday. My father held my mother's hand all the way back to 1440. He didn't say anything, No one said anything.

≈✻

One night, after Grandma Wade had finally gone, and David and I had our room back, I was listening to my parents getting ready for bed, a comforting routine during which I usually fell asleep. In my dozy state, I heard my mother mention my father's employer and Jack O'Brien in the same sentence. I roused and stared up into the shadows cast by the hall light, rehearing her words in my head, wondering why Arthur Woodhull had cautioned my father to be careful and why that troubled my mother. Until all of the uproar, it had never occurred to me that my father's support of Jack O'Brien might not be okay—heroic even. I was jarred by the hateful mail and phone calls and when people reproached my father openly. But to imagine that his job might be at risk, what would that mean? Could my father be punished? Might there be a price to pay even if he was doing the right thing? What would that be like?

That night, from my bed, as I heard my father calming my mother's worries, I imagined him patting her reassuringly or kissing her on the forehead. I heard his calming voice whispering to her before the light in their room went out. From that moment on, the thing that was troubling my mother, the fragile nature of security, of being safe, became mine as well. Up until then, I hadn't connected my father's work with food, clothes, or the shelter of old 1440. His job was just what he did. Every day he went off to the mortuary. My mother stayed home and did her work, and David and I did what kids do. For the rest of that summer, I felt a sense of relief each day when my father left the house for work. We were secure for another day.

But apprehension over my father's preoccupation with Jack O'Brien had taken root. I began to think differently about the man in the cell. I began to question his innocence. What if he was guilty after all? Where would we live if Mr. Woodhull fired my father because Jack O'Brien turned out to be the killer? Could my father be arrested for saying the killer was innocent when he wasn't?

For a time after that, each day was a bit of torture for me. Days would go by when I ignored the freedom of summer. I stayed close to home. I would go to the library and bring back a stack of books and sit inside reading. My mother's attempts to lure me outside were shunned. I had to be in the house; 1440 was security. I asked my father every morning when he would be coming home and when that time drew near, I would put my book aside and be waiting for him on the bridge. When he smiled I knew he still had a job. For once, I wasn't interested in hearing him talk about Jack O'Brien. I even quit reading the evening paper.

≋✷

Grandma Wade's encampment had lasted six days. It seemed like a month. She was my grandmother and all, but I grew tired of sleeping on the shifting cushions of our couch and of the tension that hung in the air. The hateful letters and vulgar phone calls began during her stay, and we all had to endure her gasps and chagrin at the *whole affair*. I remember walking around with this fake smile on my face and always knocking on the bathroom door before going in just in case because of the time I'd caught Grandma Wade sitting on the toilet with her cotton underpants down around her feet. For some time afterwards, I had nightmares of the snarling shriek she gave me.

She left on a Saturday morning about ten. We all smilingly saw her off, and my father rode with her in the taxi to the bus depot then walked home to save cab fare. By the time he came through the front door, David and I had reclaimed our space. I was lying on my bed thumbing through a Red Ryder comic, enjoying the familiar feel of it, when I felt him standing in the open doorway. After a moment he came in and sat on the edge of my mattress. He didn't say anything right off, just took off his glasses, fogged them with his breath and swabbed the lenses with a handkerchief. He carefully slipped the curved hook of each bow over his ears and settled the frame onto his nose.

"Glad to have your room back?" he asked after studying me. I nodded, and he smiled. "Tired of sleeping on the couch?" I nodded again. "Well, I know your grandmother appreciated your sacrifice. But I did put her on the bus, Philip. She is gone. I promise." He held up his hand like he was taking an oath. I smiled, and he reached out and ruffled my hair. "I've missed seeing that smile," he said, "are you okay?"

"Yeah, guess so."

"Guess so? Why guess so?"

"I don't know. I mean, yeah, I'm okay."

He reached out and tapped my skull with a forefinger. "What's going on in there? Your mother says you hardly go out of the house. Reading all the time."

"I like to read."

My father sat back, folded his arms, and lowered his chin. "What is it?"

I flipped the pages of the comic book, then laid it on my stomach. "Dad? Are you sure about Jack O'Brien? I mean, that he isn't the one, you know, the one who killed Mrs. Dugan?"

He drew his lips in. "Am I still certain that he's innocent? Is that what's on your mind?" When I nodded he said, "Son, I am absolutely certain that Jack has been falsely accused. Not a doubt in my mind."

"But what if he did it, and you lose your job? Where would we live?"

My father dropped his arms and stared at me. "What? Whatever put such a thought in your head, Philip?"

"You said Mr. Woodhull didn't like you standing up for Jack," I blurted. "You did, Dad. He'll fire you, won't he, if Jack did it?"

"Of course not. For heaven's sake. Here, sit up now." He pulled me up by my shoulders and looked me straight in the eye. "No matter how things turn out with Jack O'Brien, I would never put you and David and your mother at risk. You come first—always." He shook me gently. "You understand that?"

I nodded.

"Good, let's hope so."

"Dad," I said, "is Jack sad about being in jail?"

"Sad? I expect so. It's no fun being locked up, especially for something you didn't do."

"Can I see him?"

My father looked at me and pulled at his nose and stroked his chin. "I don't think so, son. The only people allowed to see him are his lawyer and family. They only let me in because Jack doesn't have any family here."

"Could I write to him?" I said.

My father pondered, nodding his head. "I think so. Can't see why not."

"And you could deliver it right to him. Couldn't you?"

"I sure could." He was grinning.

That afternoon, I wrote my first letter to Jack O'Brien.

Dear Jack O'Brien,

I am Philip Wade. Maybe you remember me. You helped my dad put a roof on our house. It is a good roof. It never leaks. Thank you for the good roof. I hope you are okay. Do you have a bed?

Your friend, Philip

My father said the letter was just fine, that he was sure Jack O'Brien would appreciate it. My mother gave me an envelope, and my father took my letter with him when he next visited Jack O'Brien. Of course, I fell on my father after his visit to the jail and swamped him with questions about giving Jack O'Brien the letter. Yes, he'd given it to him. Did he read it? Not right then. Did he say anything about getting it? Not right then. Was he going to write back? No idea. I waited and tortured my father every time he saw him, until I decided that Jack O'Brien wasn't going to write back.

So what, I reasoned. Not everything hinged on Jack O'Brien. To heck with him. Summer was in full bloom, and other things were going on that weren't about Katherine Dugan or Jack O'Brien, like the roaring assaults on Reservoir Hill. Men from around town would try to gun their cars and trucks up the slope, them against the hill. Often in the early evening men in Buicks and Jeeps, even motorcycles, would take a run at the hillside, going all out to get to the top. None ever did, at least that I saw.

After dinner one evening, I heard an engine roaring and ran to the front yard and saw an olive green Dodge Power Wagon with all four of its big bumpy tires churning up dirt and rocks on the incline. On the stubby truck's first run, the engine bogged down and almost died. The driver backed down the embankment, brought the engine's rpm's back up with a roar, and chunked back into gear. It was gravity against machine, and it seemed that the big Dodge would beat the hillside. Dust flew, the nose of the vehicle crept up the slope, but all at once the driver cut the throttle and backed off. The Power Wagon idled for a bit as the dust settled, then the unknown driver backed away and drove southeast out of town. I watched until it went out of sight. All I had seen of the driver was a bare forearm resting on the window sill.

-11-

The end of July came. Jack O'Brien was still in jail. Because it was a murder case, and the accused was unemployed, had no local ties, and the district attorney argued that he might flee if released, no bail had been set. My father fretted and fumed daily, because nothing was happening. He and Haskin MacHall had become, if not friends, mutually respectful of each other. They met often, sometimes at the attorney's office, but mostly at our house. For a time, the blue Packard had a permanent parking place at our house.

At first, MacHall was noticeably reluctant to talk in front of me. Then, without comment, he was no longer hesitant. I suspect that my father said something to clear the way. Still, I could tell the attorney didn't like me being present when they had to speak frankly about Jack and the murder and legal tactics. To him, I was a kid who would surely run off at the mouth; he didn't know I'd never say anything.

Two months after Mrs. Dugan's murder, public sentiment still ran deep and vengeful. The arrest of Jack O'Brien had temporarily quelled the most outspoken fears and outrage of Baker City residents. The authorities wanted to keep it that way. They were in no hurry to conclude the investigation of their prime suspect.

On Monday, August 2, seventy-two days after the killing, my father and Haskin MacHall met again. It was early evening when MacHall arrived, and they reviewed the status of O'Brien's confinement over coffee. I sat at the opposite end of the couch from the attorney and ignored him the way he ignored me.

"Ken, they just aren't going to budge—not yet." MacHall shook his head, loosened his tie, and slipped out of his suit coat. He looked tired.

"They've had Jack on ice for a month. Don't they have to do something?"

MacHall shrugged. "They have: They've arrested him for murder, and they're taking their time building the case. Frankly, and not to over emphasize my own influence, I thought when I came into the picture they would be inclined to fish or cut bait. Well, they're just making more bait."

"It's all circumstantial." My father had said that a hundred times. "You said so yourself."

MacHall nodded patiently. "Yeah, but they think they can connect all that to hard facts. People want this solved. Now. Women are adamant." He looked over at me, held silent for a moment, but went ahead. "Ever since the Lilly Marks murder the women in this town have been afraid to be out after dark. Then, we get this, the Dugan killing. People want justice, and O'Brien's as good as the next suspicious character."

"Makes a lot of sense," my father said. "But the real murderer is still out there. Silly to think holding Jack makes them safe."

"I know, sounds idiotic, but not if they think they have the real guy. Look at what they have, circumstantial or not. First, they have a lead from a citizen."

"Come on, Haskin," my father protested. "Velma Lumpkin is a screwball. She's not credible."

MacHall shrugged. "Maybe so, but they still have Jack's intimidating presence." With each incriminating fact, he jabbed a forefinger into the palm of his hand. "They have proximity. They have bloody evidence. They have his wound. They have possible weapons. They have a suspicious lifestyle. And the accused has no alibi for his whereabouts during the time in question."

"What about motive? Nothing was stolen. What possible reason could Jack have had?"

MacHall looked my way again then said, "Attempted assault would be my guess."

"You mean...?"

"Yes, I mean."

"Balderdash." My father looked over at me, too. There was something they weren't saying out loud for me to hear. "There was no evidence to support such a charge."

"Could be when they present their case."

"Are they looking at the possibility of other suspects?"

MacHall shook his head. "Not that I know of, and my contacts are very good, Ken. They're just happy as hell to have O'Brien between them and public outcry while they put a fence around the guy."

"He didn't do it," I whispered what I was thinking. When Mr. MacHall slowly turned his head toward me, I leaned back against the cushion. His face was slack, and he studied me like I'd just farted or something. I could see in his eyes that I'd confirmed his point; I was only a kid, a mouthy kid.

My father pointed a finger at me and shook his head. "And what are we doing, Haskin? Are we building a defense?"

"There's not much I can do. O'Brien can't account for his whereabouts that night. The guy's a loner. He can't prove he's been anywhere at any time—ever. Except when he helped you with the roof. So, Ken, you tell me. If I say, hey the man is innocent. He was just out for a walk. *And where was he walking,* they ask. Oh, down by the river. *And where was the crime committed?*" MacHall raised his arms. "I rest my case. No, the best thing we can do is make them present their case, challenge their evidence, and take it apart piece by piece."

"But you do believe him," said my father.

MacHall leaned forward, elbows on his knees and clasped his hands. "Mostly, yes."

"Mostly?"

"Look. Like I've said, Ken, I am not a fan of the way this guy lives. I mean just hanging around, squatting on city property, no job. It's just not the way real people live. He gives some people the creeps. Like my wife."

My father squinted through his round gold rims. "But you are going to see this thing through, aren't you, Haskin?"

There was a slight pause. "Sure. For now, sure."

"For now?"

"Yes, for now." MacHall stood and cinched up his tie. "Due to your urging,

Ken, I looked into this. Like you, I wanted to make sure that my town wasn't railroading an innocent man. And I'm mostly convinced that Jack didn't do this thing. But if the state crime lab connects up any of their evidence, I may have to rethink my position. In fact, I have to tell you that's what I've promised my law partners. A look-see is one thing. Commitment to a wrong cause is another."

I watched my father get up from his chair, his jaw clenching. He waited as MacHall slipped his coat back on. "Do you have any idea what it's like to sit in a jail cell knowing you're innocent," he asked, "but also knowing that outside the walls you have been declared guilty of something heinous, and people believe you did it? Do you know how that feels, Haskin? How hopeless Jack feels right now? So while you're playing hide and seek with your public image, there's a man in a cage whose only hope is that we will not quit on him."

Haskin MacHall sniffed and looked unperturbed. "I know you're committed, Ken. I'd want you in my corner if it came to that, so I'm going to overlook your implications regarding my integrity. Get some rest."

"This can go bad, you know," my father said. His voice had gone flat. "I've seen it happen. Being locked up. Fearing that people want you dead can make a man desperate."

"Meaning?"

"What do you think?"

"Oh come now, Ken. Jack'll be okay." MacHall looked in my direction then reached down to pick up his briefcase. "I've got something for you," he said to me. He never said my name. "Jack asked me to give you this."

He held out a sheet of folded paper between two fingers like it was unclean. I thanked him and forced myself to stand quietly, even though the paper was burning in my hand. My father stood at the front door window and watched the Packard drive away. He stood that way for a couple of minutes, patted me on the back, and went into the kitchen and poured himself some coffee.

Later that evening, after I had read and reread my letter from Jack O'Brien, I found my father sitting in his chair holding the ledger book he used for his poetry, writing short lines in his wide scrawl. My mother sat in her chair darning socks; she smiled at me, but nothing was said. When I went to bed, he was still there under the lamp, pen in hand. He was troubled, and I'd half-expected him to go out for one of his walks.

Before turning off the light by my bed, I read the letter one more time.

Dear Philip,

Thank you for the letter. I am glad that the roof is keeping you dry. It was a good day when your father and I did that job. Yes, I do have a bed, a cot really. It is hard but I like it that way. I hope you are having a good summer. Summertime was always fun for me when I was your age. I miss those days. You take care now.

Your friend, Jack O'Brien

P. S. Always remember what a fine man your father is.

I'd shown my parents the letter at the dinner table. They both read it, exchanged looks, and told me that it was a fine letter. When I asked if I could write to Jack O'Brien again, there was a long silence before my mother said she didn't think it would be a good idea. But my father shrugged, avoided my mother's questioning eyes, and said he didn't think it would hurt.

"A little innocent correspondence might be good for Jack."

"I don't think it's healthy," my mother said, "Philip writing to a man who's in jail."

"I don't see the harm," my father said.

"I know." My mother began clearing the table.

After I agreed that my parents had to approve anything I wrote to Jack O'Brien before it was delivered to him, I was given permission to write again.

≋⋆

Two days later, Walt Disney's new movie *Bambi* opened at the Empire Theater. My father had the night off, so the whole family went to see it. It was the first time we had been out on the town since moving to Baker City. The theater was packed with families. On the way home, my mother had to keep explaining to David that it was just a story, that Bambi's mother didn't really die. But I thought to myself, if you believed the story, she did.

When we walked in the door, the phone was ringing. Mother answered and nodded to herself. "Yes, just a moment, Mr. MacHall." She held the receiver out to my father.

"Haskin? No, we just walked in. Took the boys to see *Bambi*. Yes, they liked it, great movie. What can I do for you?" My father sat on an arm of the overstuffed chair and stared at the floor, listening. "When was this supposed to have happened? Uh-huh. He woulda been what, about sixteen? Yeah. So how does that...? What? No. You're not serious." My father stood up suddenly. "Come on now, I can't believe...Sorry? I'm sure you are, but that doesn't help Jack. You bet I'm disappointed. Is that final? I see. Huh? Well, that's something. Yes, I'll call when that happens. Yeah, me, too. Good-bye."

He held the receiver in his hand for a long moment before hanging it up. When he turned, we were all staring at him, waiting. It was quiet. The Kelvinator refrigerator was humming in the kitchen. In an instant, my father had lost his vigor; he looked depleted. He lowered himself into his chair and stuck his legs out.

"What?" my mother asked. "Ken?"

"Well," he sighed, "MacHall is pulling out. Quitting on us." He said a curse word under his breath and looked up at his wife. "When he was here last time the signals were pretty clear that he'd quit if he could find a way. Now he has."

"So, he's guilty after all," my mother said a bit too quickly.

My father squinted a frown. "Is that what you want? So he'll be out of our lives?" He sighed. "Never mind, can't say as I blame you."

"Yes, I do want this mess over with—and out of our lives. It's a nightmare. But do I want him to be wrongly found guilty? No." She looked down at her husband. "So what did Haskin say?"

"The district attorney found Haskin's ticket out when he conducted a search of old county records for anything he could find on Jack. Turns out that when Jack was sixteen, he was charged with assault. Beat up some kid pretty bad, and they sent him to MacLaren School for Boys in Woodburn for six months."

"Sixteen? He was just a boy," said my mother. "What was it about?"

My father scrubbed his face with the palms of his hands. "Jack's father died when he was a teenager. Remember me telling you? Ran into a bridge abutment one night in November in 1928, I think. Killed instantly. Drunk."

David had fallen asleep on the couch beside me. My mother covered him with an afghan then moved behind my father's chair and began to massage his shoulders. "What's that have to do with now?" she asked.

My father grunted beneath my mother's probing fingers. "My question exactly. Damn it, how did I get into this mess?"

"My question exactly," said my mother, still massaging.

Her sarcasm went unacknowledged.

My father closed his eyes. "Anyway," he breathed, "Haskin said that Jack's juvenile record verifies his violent tendencies. Guess some kid made remarks about Jack's dad being a drunk, so Jack beat him within an inch. By his measuring stick, that's all Haskin needed to get out from under this thing. Promised his law partners he would if something surfaced that makes Jack look more likely. Well, got his wish."

My mother kept kneading the back of his neck. "Does that give you pause?"

My father's eyes remained closed. "Do I think because Jack flew off the handle as a kid, he'd do it again? Are you hoping my mind will be changed as easily as Haskin's, Margaret?"

"Oh, stop," she said. "Quit being the martyr. Warney can't hear you."

I had been only half-listening, but I rose up from slouching on the couch when I heard Warney's name come from my mother's mouth. My father reached behind his neck and took hold of her wrists and got up from the chair. He turned to face her still holding on. They stood like that for a long moment; then, he left the house by the front door. I watched out the side window as he walked off down the road toward the river. When he came back an hour or so later, I was listening to Jack Benny on the radio. He went right to bed without saying a word. My mother puttered around in the kitchen until long after I'd gone to bed.

The house was quiet when I got up the next morning. David was still sleeping, my mother was loading the washer, and my father had already left for work. I ate a bowl of Cheerios and thought about what to do with the day. My interest in cornering the drive-by refreshment market had expired with my Kool-Aid stand's one-day run. I didn't feel like going to the river or playing with the neighbor kids. I had decided to go to the library when my mother came in and told me to stick around and run the vacuum cleaner.

So there I sat, floating the last three Cheerios in a puddle of milk, pushing them down with my spoon and watching them stubbornly bob up again, when a booming knock rattled the front door. I heard my mother's brisk steps then her voice rise in a greeting. My trance broken, I wandered in to find Uncle Chet standing in the living room, cap in hand. With him was a man some years older, less robust and with a slight stoop. The man doffed a gray fedora and smiled at my mother.

"Margaret, this here's my friend, Oscar Doolittle. Oscar, this is my cousin's wife, Margaret, and that there's Philip." Uncle Chet went into a bowlegged boxer's stance and gently jabbed me on the arm.

The other man tipped his head to my mother and shook her hand then waved to me. He appeared more lively up close. His eyes were clear blue beneath a thin and nearly all white receding hairline. He wore a light gray suit set off by a bright, red-and-white polka dot bow tie.

"Please be seated," my mother gestured. "Can I get you some coffee, Chet? Mr. Doolittle?"

"Oh, no, Margaret. We'll be here just a bit. Is Ken around?"

She looked between them. "No. He's at work. Something I can tell him?"

Uncle Chet rubbed a hand through the few wispy strands of white hair he still had. "Well, I know Ken's been doing his darnedest to get that there Jack O'Brien some legal help. Damn proud of him too, I say. You know, visiting him in jail and getting that lawyer to look into things. Good work."

My mother nodded. Mr. Doolittle looked into his hat as Uncle Chet rattled on.

"Anyhow, rumor has it that Haskin MacHall's done quit on him. That right?"

"Why…yes," my mother responded, "but how do you know that? Just happened last night."

Uncle Chet smiled. "Luck of the draw, Honey. You see, Oscar and me, we have coffee together most every morning over to the Inland Cafe. That place is a mess of truckers, businessmen and the like—every morning." He glanced at Oscar Doolittle. "Well, this morning, Margaret, you're not gonna believe this. Anyway, we're sitting in our usual booth, right by the front door, you know, where we can watch the comings and goings. Well sir, there was this fella practically had his coat sleeve in my coffee cup—standing that close he was—fella the name of Benjamin Taylor."

"Travis," corrected Doolittle, "Benjamin Travis."

"Right, that's right, Travis." He raised his eyebrows and leaned forward. "Of MacHall, Travis and MacHall. Well, this Travis is so close I can smell his shaving soap, and he's making small talk with some other fella. Didn't know him. Anyway, what's his name, Travis, being as discreet as a belch in church, lets it out that his firm is no longer representing Jack O'Brien. Exact words was, 'Best we're out of it—not going anywhere'. Right there bold as brass." Uncle Chet sat back, smiling and slapped Oscar Doolittle on the knee, causing the man to wince. "So, here we are."

I guess it dawned on me and my mother about the same time. We looked at each other and tried not to smile. This was *the* Oscar Doolittle. The very lawyer my father had poked fun at.

Uncle Chet sat there grinning and nearly twisting his old cap into a rope until he spit it out. "Here's the thing, Margaret. O'Brien's gonna be needing a new lawyer, won't he, now?" My mother hesitated then nodded carefully. Uncle Chet flopped back and gave poor Mr. Doolittle another blow to the knee. "Here's your man."

≋✻

Before I knew it, I was on my way to the funeral home. I marched with some urgency past the Post Office, but once in front of that big house, my resolve began to falter. I had never been inside the place where my father did certain things to people who'd had a misfortune. The prospect of going in there was something I'd always thought of with my father by my side. I stood on the porch getting up my courage; then I turned the brass doorknob and stepped inside. I inhaled. The air had a sweetness to it, I guessed from thousands of sad bouquets. The carpet was the color of cranberry sauce. I walked across it gingerly into the entry way, past white pillars and a staircase that curved up out of sight. When no one came out, I wandered into the first open doorway looking for my father. The entire room was filled with caskets, every lid yawning open.

My heart rolled, and I held my breath, certain that there would be an unfortunate body in each one. But they were all empty, merely on display like a furniture store. All that was missing was a sign declaring: *Use Our Convenient Lay Away Plan*. I peered into the casket next to me—light blue with silver-gray handles and a ruffled, vanilla white interior. It looked so plush and comfortable. I put my hand inside and pushed on the tufted pillow—it was not as soft as it looked. Guess it didn't have to be.

My hand was still resting on the pillow when my back felt prickly and I knew someone else was there. As calmly as I could muster, I pulled my hand out of the ruffles and turned. My father stood in the doorway, his suit coat on. We both had surprised looks on our faces.

"Philip," he said, like we hadn't seen each other for months. "What…is something wrong?"

"No. But Mom was wondering if you could come home early for lunch."

My father frowned and looked at his watch. "Sure. I guess so. What's up?"

"Uncle Chet's at our house with another man."

"Another man?"

"Yeah," I smiled. "Oscar Doolittle, remember?"

He did. He went home early for lunch.

-12-

Uncle Chet and Oscar Doolittle were still sitting in our living room entertaining my mother when my father and I burst into the house. My mother was laughing so hard at something Uncle Chet had said that her face was rosy. The men stood up from the couch in unison and exchanged head-bobbing and handshakes with my father before we all adjourned to the kitchen. My mother put out the fixings for bologna and cheese sandwiches and a pitcher of lemonade. She busied herself at the table for a few minutes then left, closing the kitchen door and making no attempt to exclude me from the gathering. By then, she knew I was a lost cause.

I stood captivated by the awkwardness of the men slathering mayonnaise onto slices of white bread, positioning Velveeta slices and rounds of bologna. They were making something to eat, not to admire. None of them used the lettuce leaves my mother had put out, so I didn't either. Uncle Chet made the ugliest sandwich of all while taking sidelong peeks at my father.

"Margaret, she's not happy 'bout this I gather," Uncle Chet said tipping his head toward the closed door.

My father shrugged, poured himself some lemonade, and sat down.

"Ruth's grumpy, too. Thinks I ought not to be meddling in this thing. You either. Mess she calls it. Terrible mess."

"She's right about that," my father said and took a bite out of his sandwich.

"Damned sorry to hear about MacHall quitting on you."

My father shrugged again, took another bite and chewed quietly.

"Cowardly, if you ask me." Uncle Chet was squinting.

"Just business," my father said. "Nothing I can do about it."

Uncle Chet leaned toward my father. "Still, mighty proud of you." He reached a long arm out and slapped my father on the back. "Yessir. Right, Oscar?"

Before Oscar Doolittle could respond, my father said, "Okay, Chet, what's going on? What you got up your sleeve?"

The old man rubbed the white hair on his burly forearm.

"Got no sleeves," he laughed. "But okay, yeah. Me and Oscar here been thinkin'. Jack's gonna need a new lawyer—right?"

My father peeked at Oscar Doolittle, who was taking small bites of his sandwich. "Well," he said, "it's getting desperate. Jack's no closer to getting out of jail. He's innocent, Chet. Damnation. Man sits all alone in a jail. Terrified that he's being made out a killer. Thinking he doesn't have a chance. It's not going to happen again. Warney didn't do this." My father's face was pink.

The two men were staring at my father, puzzled expressions on their faces.

"Who's Warney?" asked Uncle Chet.

My father blinked, put his sandwich down, and leaned back.

"You okay, Ken?"

"I said Warney?"

Uncle Chet nodded, and my father looked at each of us in turn.

I smiled, and he reached out and gripped my arm for an instant.

"Warney was my best friend growing up. He hung himself in a jail cell. Just like now, there was a killing, and he was locked up on circumstantial evidence." He sat massaging his hands. "I don't want that to happen again."

"Ken, we're gonna lick this."

My father tried to smile. "Convince me."

Uncle Chet turned to Oscar Doolittle and laid a hand on the man's back. "Starting right here. Oscar is an old geezer like me, but he's a damn good lawyer."

My father studied the hunched over old man with the blue eyes and polka dot tie. I couldn't quite read his expression; it was either one of despair or longing.

"Okay," Uncle Chet plopped his hands down on the table. "Let's get down to brass tacks. First off, Oscar, here, is 78 years old. Eight years older'n me. Older than dirt. So old, in fact, he once worked with Clarence Darrow hisself."

My father's eyebrows arched up. I didn't know who Clarence Darrow was then, but, obviously, he was someone significant. "Clarence Darrow?"

"That's right." Uncle Chet sat back and thumped the table with the meaty part of a fist. "Okay if I tell on you a bit, Oscar?"

The old man nodded politely and took a sip of lemonade. "A bit."

"Okay. Well, when Oscar was just a virgin out of law school in Chicago, he wangled himself a job with Darrow. Right when George Pullman—the railroad car builder—right when old George and Eugene V. Debs got into a donnybrook. 'Member Debs? The fella that begun the American Railway Union? That one. Anyway, when Pullman's workers got fed up with his unfair layoffs, poverty wages, and company-owned-town graft, they joined up with Debs' union. So old Pullman fired his workers who were leaders of the local union. But then all of his workers went on strike.

"Hell of a mess. Grover Cleveland sent federal troops. Debs refused a court order to quit the strike, so he and seven other Union officials was arrested and tried. The newspapers named 'em the 'Woodstock Eight'. Darrow was their lawyer and sitting by his side was a young buck name of Oscar Quincy Doolittle."

"And we lost." Oscar Doolittle smiled, his blue eyes dancing. "All eight of those men were convicted and spent six months in the Woodstock, Illinois, jail."

My father laughed. I could tell he was beginning to warm to Mr. Doolittle.

"Now wait a minute, Ken." Uncle Chet wasn't done. "I want to make my point here. Oscar went on to become a big labor law attorney in the Washington of D.C."

Oscar Doolittle snorted out a laugh. "Getting a little deep in here."

My father smiled back. "So why Baker City?"

"Born here. Sold out to my law partners and moved back to the family ranch. We've raised beef since the late 1800s. Couple of younger brothers run the place. My wife's gone, no children, so I built a little place on one corner of the ranch and just putter now. Just an old curmudgeon keeping his hand in and stirring up things whenever I can. Other than that, Chet and I go to the Inland Café, drink coffee and tell lies."

Uncle Chet folded his arms across his chest. "Okay, enough palaver—let's talk about getting Jack O'Brien out of the slammer."

So then and there, over bologna sandwiches, it was agreed. Oscar Quincy Doolittle would be retained as Jack O'Brien's attorney—if Jack agreed—and for the same fee as MacHall, one dollar. Uncle Chet promptly laid a single bill on the table and smoothed it out with his hands. I saw my father's dejection begin to roll over. He shook Oscar Doolittle's hand and repeated his belief in Jack O'Brien's innocence. Fingering his bow tie, the attorney quietly commented that as corny as it may sound, justice is about truth. If it was true that Jack O'Brien wasn't responsible for Katherine Dugan's death, then justice would set him free. He said that Darrow had a quote that he had referred to often over the years: *Chase after the truth like hell, and you'll free yourself, even though you never touch its coattails.*

While the old men sought out my mother to thank her for the lunch, my father made himself another sandwich and sat eating it with a pleased look on his face. He winked at me and reached over to ruffle my hair once again. The lines of gloom were gone. It was then I realized just how responsible he felt for Jack O'Brien. Of course, I'd seen his anger and his fussing about the plight of a man being wronged. Looking back on it now, I know a lot of it *was* about atoning for what had happened to Warney Webster. He didn't really know Jack O'Brien; there was no real connection between them, other than roofing nails. When he sat in his chair of an evening and stared off, I had always figured he was thinking of a man in a cell, alone, certain no one cared—but which face was in his head, that of Jack O'Brien or Warney Webster? My father had for certain taken on the crusade for Jack O'Brien to purge old nightmares. Regardless, I was glad to have him smiling again.

When he had finished his second sandwich, my father went looking for my mother and found her in the living room going through sheet music for choir practice that night. He went over to her as she sat on the piano bench, wrapped his arms around her from behind, and kissed her on the neck. She wiggled and laughed as music sheets cascaded off her lap onto the floor.

"Ken, stop," she sang out unconvincingly. "What on earth are you doing?"

"Having dessert after two bologna sandwiches. And very sweet, I might add."

My mother smiled and looked over at me, and her neck turned red. I liked it when my father messed around like that.

"Dare I ask why you're so wound up?" she said and began retrieving the jumble of sheet music from the floor.

"Doolittle is going to help us."

She looked up. "You mean the do-very-little Doolittle?"

"I know, I know. But, Margaret, the guy once worked with Clarence Darrow. He was a big time national labor law attorney. Don't let the stoop and gray hair fool you. We're back on track." My father clapped his hands and rubbed them together.

"That so?" My mother slipped the sheets of music into her leather case. "Before you go back to work, I'd like to talk with you."

"About what?"

"What else?"

My father dropped into the armchair and looked up at his wife innocently. "Okay. Shoot."

"Just us this time."

"Uh, all right," my father said with a nod. "Philip, Mom and I need to talk. Okay? How about you go outside for a bit."

"Why?" I felt betrayed. "I know all about Jack O'Brien."

My mother shook her head at me. "It's not just that, Philip. Sometimes husbands and wives need to talk just between the two of them. That's the way it is this time." She saw my dismay. "Why don't you run to the store and get some milk. We're about out."

My father held out two quarters, and they waited, saying nothing. Flaming with anger, I snatched the coins and charged out, slamming the front door. I ran all the way to Freddie Patterson's and burst into the store, nearly colliding with a woman carrying a paper sack in each arm. She let out a whoosh of surprise and sputtered something. I mumbled an apology and turned to see Pearl Dorsey thumbing through a comic book grinning at me. My anger evaporated in an instant, and I was under the spell of this energetic creature in her white tee-shirt and dungarees.

"Hey, Philip. Fall in, why don'tcha?"

I blushed and stammered something and rushed to pull a quart bottle of milk from the cooler. I waited while she finished her shopping, and we left together. She walked easily in the early afternoon heat, holding the paper grocery sack in front of her, both arms wrapped around it. I tried to match her long, liquid strides.

"So," she said with that bright edge to her voice, "how was the lemonade stand? Make lots of money?"

"Nah, just did it for one day. It was only Kool-Aid, anyway."

"Well, when I went by, looked like you had a lot of business."

I smiled. Her praise was an elixir. "Guess I did all right."

"So," she said kind of slow and low, "your dad still helping that guy? The one in jail?"

"Jack O'Brien?"

"Yeah. Him. The one that's supposed to have killed the teacher."

As much as I was goo-goo over her, I felt an itch at the back of my neck from her questions. I didn't take her bait, just hugged the cool bottle of milk closer and stared down at the sidewalk. After a bit, she jostled her grocery sack, getting a new grip on it, and looked down at me—I could feel her eyes.

"What do you think? Think he killed her?"

I kicked at a pebble on the sidewalk and muffed it. I stepped back, kicked at it again, and connected, sending it dancing out into the street.

"Well," she probed, "do you, Philip?"

I stopped walking and turned to face her, defiantly looking up into her questioning brown eyes. "No," I said. "He didn't do it."

She blinked. "But how do you know? They say he did it. The police—I mean—they say he's guilty."

"I just know. Jack wouldn't hurt anybody."

We stopped at the walk in front of the Dorsey house, a two-story with white siding and a big front porch with a swing on it. Two bicycles lay on their sides in the yard. Pearl adjusted her grip on the grocery bag. "I guess you could be right," she said. "But a lot of people think he probably did it. Even my parents. I sure hope…"

I started walking and didn't look back. I heard Pearl call my name, but I didn't stop. My eyes burned. I was mad. Mad at Pearl Dorsey, mad at Jimmy Purdue, mad at Mr. MacHall—and mad at my father. Everybody thought Jack O'Brien was guilty and that my father was a fool. Everywhere I went, people we knew looked at us differently and made small talk. I just knew that when we were out of sight they talked differently. Those dumb Wades! That's what made me mad and embarrassed. But stubborn, too, even if it was a struggle to be proud of my father and humiliated at the same time. Pearl's accusations hurt the most.

-13-

I trudged resolutely back home, turning righteous anger over in my mind as I held the warming bottle of milk in my arms. Indignation turned to foreboding when I found my father sitting out on the front steps reading the evening paper. He peered calmly at me over the headlines as I slowed to a shuffle coming up the walk, eyeballed whatever he had been reading one more time, then refolded the paper carefully.

"Here, let me have that," he said reaching out for the bottle of milk. "Sit down."

I sat beside him, waiting and wondering why he hadn't gone back to work yet. This was not good. After setting the milk bottle behind him, he picked up the folded newspaper and rolled it into a tube. My stomach murmured warnings to me.

"Philip." My stomach really jerked when he said my name, slow and serious. "I'm disappointed. Your mother and I needed a few moments alone. Sometimes we need to talk, just the two of us."

"But…"

"Be still. Listen." He tapped the rolled paper into his hand. "Just listen. I know you think it was about Jack O'Brien, and you should be in on every discussion of him. Maybe it was about that. Makes no difference. We're the parents—not you. I thought you'd grown up a bit. Guess I was wrong." He looked over at me. "You were angry when you left for the store, weren't you?"

I shrugged my shoulders. "A little, maybe."

"Well," my father patted the rolled paper into his hand a couple of more times, "in your outburst, you broke one of your mother's dishes. You slammed the door, and one of her nicest dishes fell."

A sizzling sensation ran up my spine and electrified the back of my neck.

He spoke as if there had been a misfortune in the family. "What do you think I should do about that?"

So we quietly discussed my fate, the menu of various forms of punishment available to me. The fate of Jack O'Brien moved into the background. My father didn't look at me as we debated the merits of washing dishes for a year versus an immediate laying on of his belt. A neighbor walked by, and my father matched the man's perfunctory wave. It was but a momentary reprieve. I had to decide my own sentence. I chose the immediate pain.

With that my father stood, put a hand on my shoulder, and guided me into the house to the torture chamber of my bedroom. My mother met us in the living room, took the milk bottle from my father and disappeared into the kitchen—it had all been arranged. We entered my bedroom where I received four whacks of my father's belt, laid on with force befitting the wrong. My posterior did burn, and tears did well up, more from humiliation than pain. Afterward, my father methodically fed his belt back through the loops on his pants and left me to my mortification. I hid out in the quiet of the bedroom for quite awhile, long after the stinging from the belt had subsided. I was still lying on my bed, hands folded on my stomach, when David burst into the room wearing a cowboy hat and carrying his Red Ryder cap pistol. He stood very still, holding the toy weapon at his side, and looked at me from under that silly hat, his eyes open wide, staring and curious.

"Did you get spanked?"

I nodded.

"Did it hurt?"

"Not much," I lied.

David stuck the toy pistol into his holster. "Mom's really sad about that plate. It was her most favoritest one," he dramatized, nodding as he spoke.

She was in the kitchen. I wandered in, walking stiff-legged, with my hands jammed into my pockets. She was standing at the counter thumbing through her little wooden box of recipe cards. I went to the sink and filled a water glass. I took a couple of sips then, looking down the drain, said, "I'm sorry, Mom."

"I know you are, Philip." She put down her recipe cards and reached out to me. I was happy to have her arms around me. She tipped my chin up and smiled softly. "I'm sorry, too—sorry you had to be punished. And your father was sorry that he had to do it."

So everyone was sorry. There was enough *sorry* going around for the whole town, I thought. But I didn't want to be moping around for the next week, so I changed the subject.

"Where's Dad?" I asked.

She went back to sorting through her treasured recipe cards. "Back at work," she responded, her attention again on the next culinary project. "He'll be home for dinner and stay with you boys while I'm at choir practice. Now, run on outside and play, I have to come up with something new to do with hamburger."

I had the screen door handle in my hand, but I still didn't know what my mother had said to my father about Jack O'Brien. I decided to take another risk.

"Mom?"

"Yes." She pulled out the winning recipe and held it at arm's length.

"Do you think Dad is doing the wrong thing, about Jack O'Brien, I mean?"

She put the losing recipe cards back, set the winner aside, and closed the lid on the box. "I don't know, Philip. He thinks he's doing what has to be done."

"But do you? Some people tell me they think he's wrong, that he's protecting a killer."

At first she didn't say anything, just kept looking at the recipe card. When she did turn to me I couldn't read her feelings. "I support your father. As we all should. It is an honorable thing to stand up for someone you feel is being wronged. This will all be settled soon, and we can get back to normal. Now, scoot if you want something to eat for dinner."

I walked down Eldon Avenue, scuffing my feet in the gravel and thinking of my mother's answer to my question. She said comforting words, but her voice was toneless, like maybe she had different feelings but remained loyal to my father's views. It was confusing.

≈✿

There was no bounce in my father's step when he walked home from work that evening. He had been to see Jack O'Brien and told him about Mr. Doolittle taking on his case. O'Brien's spirits were low and only marginally lifted when told he had another lawyer. My father sat at the kitchen table and looked at the floor.

"I don't know, Margaret. I keep asking myself, how can something like this happen? Jack's like a caged wild thing that's lost its will to live."

I had my fists full of knives and forks and began setting the table. My father was massaging his hands. He did that for a long moment.

"I know what you're going to say. Don't." He didn't look at my mother when he spoke. "No matter what you think, I felt a cold dread run through me seeing him today. The man's wasting away. Gaunt. Dark circles under his eyes. He could do it. If things don't turn in his favor, no hope, he just might. When I told him we had a new attorney he just looked at me, those black eyes of his clouded. Didn't mean anything to him."

My father rubbed his hands over his face. Right then, it came to me. My father might not be able to save Jack O'Brien. Up until that point, I just assumed that this tower of strength, who could carry both David and me—one under each arm—would make it possible for O'Brien to walk out of jail a free man. But his face was slack, his eyes staring. The anger and the will to win against the odds were missing.

My mother calmly stopped what she was doing, wiped her hands on her apron, pulled him up from his slump, and began kneading his shoulders as she had done so many times. She said nothing encouraging.

Later, my father had to face Wendell Grier when he came for my mother. She was still putting on her makeup, so my father invited the choir director in to wait. They exchanged smiles; Grier's was too much and my father's was too little. I looked back and forth between them, expecting something to happen, but they just stood near the front door nursing an unspoken understanding. My father knew of Grier's disapproval, and Grier knew he did. He'd called Wendell Grier an odd duck before anyway, long before Jack O'Brien came along. When my mother didn't come out of the bedroom right away, the men were cornered, neither wanting to be the first one to speak. Grier looked around, fidgeted, then went first anyway.

"So, how's your summer going?" he asked.

My father looked at him like that was the dumbest question he had ever heard. Grier blinked a couple of times then colored a bit at the neck and pushed out an odd smile.

"Well, you know what I mean," he said.

"If you mean time off," my father said, "I won't get any. If you mean the weather, it's been great."

Grier held his wrist up and looked at his watch. "No vacation?"

"Haven't been on the job long enough."

"Oh." Grier tilted his head back. "Well, we teachers tend to forget about that."

"Must be nice," my father said.

"We earn it, let me tell you. Nine months in close quarters with thirty, and for me, sometimes sixty, kids at a time. Takes its toll. Need this time off to get my energy back." As the school district's music teacher, Mr. Grier went to every school in town teaching everything from school orchestras to choir to the high school marching band.

Now, my father looked at his watch and craned his head around as if willing my mother to emerge. "Suppose so," he said.

My father still hadn't offered Grier a seat. They stood facing one another, about six feet apart.

Grier cleared his throat, he couldn't leave it alone. "So, this

O'Brien thing, how is it going?"

"Fine," said my father.

"Terrible, just terrible. Katherine Dugan was in my choir, you know."

"I'm aware of that."

Grier nodded. "Of course." He chewed on his lip. "Pretty widespread opinion that they have the right man."

"Well, they don't have the right man."

"I know you don't think so," said Grier. "But sure seems that the case...the evidence...I mean it's all pretty convincing. Conclusive, I'd say."

"Wendell, just let it go, okay? You and I are on different sides of this. Continued discussion won't change either of us. Someone killed Katherine Dugan. That is our only agreement. And somewhere out there, that person is hoping with all of his being that Jack O'Brien will be made to pay the price for his own horrible deed."

Grier's neck reddened again, and he looked away then back. "You're being very naïve, very naïve." His voice quavered a bit. "And even irresponsible. I think you're wrong."

My father looked at the man but didn't respond. He turned at me. "Philip, go see if your mother is ready, son."

"I'm here, I'm ready," my mother said. She came into the living room with her face freshly rouged and her mouth reddened. "Shall we go, Wendell?" She walked between the two men and looked at me. I knew she had heard. But she went to the door without comment and waited for the choir director to follow. Neither man said anything more to each other.

That night, as had become my routine since Mrs. Dugan died, I laid in bed listening to my parents. I could always hear because my mother wouldn't close their door at night in case one of us boys got sick, had a scary dream or something. My eyelids were growing heavy by the time my mother had finished her nightly routine of brushing her teeth and cold-creaming her face. I had nearly drifted off when my mother said Mr. Grier's name. I raised up on my elbows to hear better.

"He was pushy," she said. "Told me lots of people in the church are critical of you. It's like his personal crusade to see that Jack O'Brien is convicted and sent to prison...or even executed." She lowered her voice at that point, but I could make out her words if I scooted up in bed.

They were so quiet, I thought the door had been closed, but then my father said, "Tonight, when he was here, I agreed that we had opposing views. I thought that would cut the tension. Guess I should have told him off in clear terms."

"Oh," my mother made the word long. "I don't know. You'd just egg him on, don't you think?"

I got out of my bed and stood by the door to hear better.

"Maybe," my father said, "but sometimes if you confront a critic, you can defang them. Take away his carnivorous tendencies."

I thought of Mr. Grier in front of the choir without any teeth, his bare gums raw and pink when he opened his mouth and waved his arms.

"All you'd do is stir him up more. Wendell is single minded, not open to changing his opinions. I know that from experience. Leave him be, Ken."

"Well, maybe you're right. But if he continues to criticize, I may call his bluff."

My father walked into the bathroom between our bedrooms, and I sat down quickly on my bed. I could see him through the slit in the half-open door wearing his white pajamas with maroon stripes. He mumbled that she shouldn't worry and began brushing his teeth as he did every night. My mother fell silent until he finished. But she began again after he flipped off the light in the bathroom. This night she seemed more wound up than usual.

"You realize, don't you, that the church is our only real connection with people in this town. We're newcomers. We don't have family here, other than the Stillmans, or a history of friends we grew up with. If we keep this up, we'll be friendless in this neighborhood. The boys will suffer at school, and we will become outcasts in our own church."

I could hear the springs on the bed give as my father slipped under the covers. "Ironic, don't you think?"

"What do you mean?"

"That the one place where we should have the benefit of not being judged is exactly the opposite? I haven't heard from John Hewett since the meeting we had here."

My mother sighed. "And I've been getting lukewarm treatment from members of the choir. I've been half-expecting Wendell to replace me as pianist." Then she laughed. "Except there isn't another decent pianist in the church—unless you count Gertrude Bowler. She would dearly love to see me out of the way."

"I've heard her play," said my father. "Those fat fingers of hers cover two keys at a time. It would be a disaster."

"Now we must be kind—mustn't we?" My mother giggled, then they both were laughing and shushing, laughing and shushing.

I laughed into my pillow, but it wasn't funny, not really.

-14-

The crummy feeling that was hanging around our house like it had squatter's rights was blown back the next day—at least for a little while. It was lunchtime. David and I were hunched over tuna sandwiches and tomato soup when my father sauntered through the back door whistling, coatless, shirt-sleeves rolled up to his elbows and tie loosened. He kissed my mother on the neck and winked at us boys.

"Enough for me?" He looked into the pot on the stove.

My mother reached into the cupboard for another bowl. "You're chipper." He sat down and took half of my sandwich and smiled when I said, "Hey!"

"Nice day out there," he said and chomped out a bite.

"It's near ninety degrees, that's what it is," my mother teased, setting a bowl of soup in front of him.

"Heat's a state of mind, just a state of mind."

"Oh," she said, "so that's what's soaking through your shirt, a state of mind. Looks like plain old sweat to me."

We all laughed. My father peppered his soup then dipped his spoon and slurped. David and I grinned and slurped right back.

He dragged out a real long slurp and smacked his lips. My mother sat down, put a napkin on her lap, and delicately slurped a spoonful herself.

"What a revolting group," my father said. "I was thinking of taking the lot of you out on the town, but…"

David and I howled our protest and my mother's eyes got shiny.

"What are you up to?" she said.

"Something…maybe."

He took another bite of my sandwich, mouthed it, and squinted at each of us in turn, eyes glinting. He rested on his elbows and began to whisper. Like puppets, we all leaned forward. *Got a call this morning.* His breathy delivery was to bedevil us. He slurped more soup then whispered, *From Mr. Lazarus McKay. Remember the McKay Ranch?*

I remembered. The people whose son had died. The first funeral my father had directed. Anyway, the McKays had invited us to be their guests at the Cattleman's Association barbecue. It would be held at the city park the following Monday, and I guessed it would be like a big party.

≋✦

When the day came, the excitement around our house was palpable. David and I fidgeted, and my mother looked at every piece of clothing in her closet twice over by the time my father got home. Then, it was time to go. The front door crashed open, and David and I plunged off of the porch and skittered out ahead of our parents for the nine blocks from our house to the city park.

From blocks away, we could smell the pungent aroma of cooking meat and see the drifting fog from the charcoal cookers. Geiser-Pollman Park was named after a miner and a butcher who had jointly given the site to the city for a public park in 1900. It was a cool grove of grass and evergreens between the Powder River on the west end and the Natatorium building on the east.

The streets were lined with cars, and the park was alive with people. A jumble of sounds met us and ran through my body like Christmas morning: A wall of adult voices, the squeals and laughter of children, the strains of live western music being played from a big band shell beneath a banner declaring, *In Memory of the American Cowboy*. A dozen or so cookers, made from 55 gallon barrels cut in half, were smoldering with slabs of beef sizzling on their grills. Behind them, men wearing cowboy hats and white aprons over their western shirts and Levi's were perspiring as they manhandled a sea of locally-raised beef steaks. Next to them, big kettles were steaming with corn on the cob and pots of pork and beans simmered and bubbled. It was a feast to my eyes and ears.

My parents and David and I all held hands and stood like paper doll cutouts until my father suddenly took off at a lope, dragging us along in his wake. My mother balked, released my father's hand, and walked with dignity to where he was shaking hands with an older man who wore a spotless, powder white Stetson. They talked like best pals while we all stood back. But it was only a moment before Mr. White Hat raised an arm and came at us like he was running for office.

"Welcome!" he sang out above the noise and lifted his hat off and dipped his head to my mother.

The grinning, bobbing, and hand squeezing felt goofy and swell at the same time. The McKay family obviously felt connected to my father. It was a scene of delight, like a huge church potluck with western music. Mrs. McKay, a striking woman with black hair and very white teeth, immediately swept up my mother, and began introducing her to the other wives. David hung onto mother's hand and leaned against her. I hung back and went with my father when Lazarus McKay struck out across the park to the food line. It seemed that nearly every man we passed knew Mr. McKay. He was greeted by big voices and vigorous handshakes; he gave back as loud and friendly as he got.

In the food line, cheery, apron-clad men loaded thick pottery plates with steaks oozing red, corn on the cob, and pork and beans. I'd never seen so much food. Balancing the overloaded plate and clutching utensils, I followed my father and Mr. McKay to a table. I sawed at my charcoal-crusted steak with little success until my father took over and sliced away several bite-sized chunks. It was so good. We were eating quietly when Haskin MacHall happened by.

"Lazarus," he said, " when a man eats without talking, the food has to be good."

Mr. McKay smiled and reached up to clasp MacHall's hand. "It is, Haskin, it truly is." He turned to my father. "Of course, you already know Ken Wade."

"Oh, sure. Hello, Ken. And Philip, how are you?"

I looked up at this smiling man, a man who had never spoken my name before and uttered a barely audible, "Fine," while I fingered the ear of corn on my plate.

"Haskin," my father said with an obligatory nod. "Good to see you."

"That so?" MacHall's laugh was quick and brittle. "I think Ken is being polite, Laz. As you may know, he and I have a point of difference over this Katherine Dugan business."

Lazarus McKay raised his eyebrows but didn't say anything in response. I saw my father's jaw clench and unclench.

"Ken's just sure Jack O'Brien is being railroaded, and I think it's more than likely that he did it. That about right, Ken?"

"All I know is a man is sitting in a jail cell terrorized, certain he is going to die for something he didn't do."

Haskin MacHall was dressed in full western garb, including cowboy boots and a brown Resistol hat. He looked like he was playing cowboy. He pulled on the brim of his hat and tensed a bit. "Be clear, Ken. Anyone accused of a crime in this county should get fair treatment, guilty or not. Don't want you implying I think otherwise. Now, I gave an impartial look at the case, and you know it. O'Brien needs counsel who believes in his case. I don't. But he'll get decent legal counsel, the court'll see to it."

"How calming to hear that," my father said. "We disagree, let's leave it at that and enjoy the festivities."

The two men were staring hard at each other, and Lazarus McKay was observing them with cool aplomb. At first, I thought Mr. MacHall was going to come back at my father. Color rose in his face, but he held his anger in check and released a sudden smile.

"Laz, always good to see you. Let's plan on a golf game soon."

"Great idea, Haskin. I haven't been out in months. Call me." The two men shook hands, and MacHall moved on and sang out a greeting to an approaching reveler.

My father watched MacHall as he moved on, then he turned to find Lazarus McKay studying him. "Sorry, Mr. McKay. Old news."

"No need to apologize. I think Haskin started it. And, please, I'm Laz to my friends."

My father nodded.

"Tell me, you really think this O'Brien's innocent?" Mr. McKay asked as he cut off another piece of steak.

"Yes," my father said, "I do."

"Why? What do you know of the man?"

My father pushed up on his glasses before he spoke. "Laz, you've been in this valley for a long time. Has there ever been occasion when you banked on a man without knowing him for very long? You know, look a man in the eye, shake his hand, and give him the keys to your bank deposit box."

McKay smiled, crinkling the skin around his eyes. "Oh, yes, I've done that a number of times. Had to."

"Did it work?"

"Yes, mostly. I once sent a man off to buy cattle for me with twenty thousand dollars in cash—all I had in the world. The cattle seller called and said he never showed. Three weeks later, the man called saying he was bringing the cattle back as planned—just a little late. Seems he was beaten up and robbed on the train. As soon as he was able, he went after the robbers. Caught up with them somewhere in Texas, put 'em both in the hospital, took the eighteen thousand still left, added two thousand of his own, and bought the cattle. He's still with me." He turned and pointed to a big man across the picnic tables. "That's him."

"Incredible," my father said.

"So I do know what you mean, Ken. That how you feel about this man O'Brien?"

"I do."

"Would you send him off with all you had?"

My father looked into the older man's eyes measuring his response. "I would."

"Well, I don't know if you're right. Haven't looked into the man's eyes like you have. But I respect your opinion."

"You're in the minority."

"Been there before."

Mr. McKay slapped my father on the back and led him over to get a beer. A cluster of men holding paper cups, laughing and talking too loud, was crowded around the beer kegs. I tagged along not wanting to miss any chance to listen in on interesting male banter. My father wasn't a big beer drinker, but on that night, he obligingly held a paper cup of beer and sipped along. I found a bucket of ice full of cold pop and pulled out a Hires root beer.

Lazarus McKay's popularity was evident wherever he went. Men in all degrees of inebriation came over to say hello, shake his hand or seize the opportunity to introduce themselves. Being with Lazarus McKay was like being in a reception line. And every person who came up had to meet my father. Most would shake his hand and look into his face and puzzle, like they should know who he was but couldn't place him.

After mingling and smiling and introducing my father—and usually me—to every person he encountered, Mr. McKay took my father by the arm and said, "Say, don't you think we ought to say hello to Mr. District Attorney? T. C. Wingate, himself. He's right over there." He leaned in closer to my father's ear and said, "By the way, the T stands for Terhune." He gave my father the impish smile of someone stirring up trouble.

My father started to object, but it was too late; McKay had already hailed the public official with a hearty shout. T. C. Wingate was a man in his mid-forties, about five-foot-nine, stocky but not fat, with rather large ears which seemed even larger because of his receding hairline and high forehead. His eyebrows were dark and bushy, slanting upward—giving him a permanent look of doubt. He had a way of holding his mouth that made it look like he was always smirking. It was quite a combination of expressions.

"T.C.," McKay said, extending and open hand, "good to see you. How's the world treating you?"

Wingate looked like he had just come from his office. He was wearing suit pants with black suspenders and dress shoes, but no coat and no tie, and his white shirt sleeves were rolled up. He gave McKay his smirky smile and took the older man's hand. "Hey, Laz. No one's treating me, I've got to earn it all. Keeping me too damn busy."

"So I hear," said McKay. He hooked a thumb in his belt and pulled at his chin. "By the way, how's that murder case coming along? You know, the schoolteacher killing?"

"Only have the one murder case, Laz. Thank god. But we have a strong case. The perpetrator's on ice, hard evidence being confirmed at the state crime lab—won't be long, and we'll go to trial. After that, I guarantee you, Mr. Jack O'Brien will get a one way ticket to Salem and the state pen courtesy of the county."

My father stood just back of McKay, and I stood just back of him. He sipped his beer and listened. I took swigs of root beer and listened. The district attorney was so puffed up with himself that he didn't notice us watching him and listening in.

"Well, sounds like you've got it cinched up, then."

Wingate unconsciously pulled down on one of his suspenders and peered into the paper cup as if something was swimming around in it.

"Let me tell you, Laz" he said. "I'll be glad to get this one over with. You won't believe the pressure I'm under to convict this guy—give him the chair." He glanced over his shoulder and lowered his voice. It was like my father and I were invisible. "It's been nonstop. The chamber, the mayor, the Elks—you name it. And those club owners that put up the five thousand—they've been unrelenting. No, the sooner I get this guy convicted and out of town, the sooner I'll be sleeping nights again."

When he finished that last sentence, he was practically whispering. I stepped closer to hear better. When I did, Wingate saw me and then my father. He drew his eyebrows in and straightened up.

Lazarus McKay turned, easy like, as innocent as could be. "Oh, pardon my manners, T.C. I'd like you to meet Ken Wade and Philip, here." He grabbed my shoulder in a clamp-like grip. "Ken works for Art Woodhull and was most helpful when we lost our son."

My father held his hand out. "Mr. Wingate." The startled district attorney quickly pulled his hand out from his suspender, which snapped back with a pop against his shirt.

"Wade." Wingate shook hands and squinted at Lazarus McKay. I took a pull on my root beer bottle and looked up at my father. He was sipping from his soggy paper cup again. Lazarus McKay broke the vacuum.

"T.C., I think Ken may have a different opinion about your case against Jack O'Brien."

Wingate squared his shoulders slightly. "Yes," he said flatly, "I know of Mr. Wade's opinion and his involvement. I happen to disagree. O'Brien is clearly guilty. You may have the best of intentions, Mr. Wade, but I think you're being naïve."

I looked around to see if the rest of the world was witnessing this drama—they weren't. What would my father do? I'd seen him very emotional about Jack O'Brien. I watched and took another drink from my bottle.

"Clearly guilty?" My father spoke calmly.

"Yes. There's no doubt," said Wingate. "I've never seen a clearer case of guilt in a murder case frankly."

"Really? And how many murder cases have you handled, Mr. Wingate?"

The district attorney paused, took a swallow of warm beer and licked his lips. "We had a similar case just two years ago," he said.

"You mean the Lilly Marks murder?"

Wingate's eyes widened, and he drew his lips into a tight line. "Yes. That's right, Lilly Marks."

Lazarus McKay waved off someone who came up to socialize. That white Stetson cast a shadow below his eyes and across the bridge of his nose. There was a force field around us. It was the strangest feeling.

"And what ever came of the Lilly Marks murder investigation?" my father asked.

Wingate shrugged. "Never solved."

My father tilted his head a bit. "I see. Any suspects?"

Wingate looked out over the park, then back to my father. "We had a couple."

"Any arrests?"

"No." Wingate's response was clipped. If Lazarus McKay hadn't been standing there taking in every word, he probably would have walked off.

"There've been others?" My father's innocent politeness brought a smile to Mr. McKay's face, which he hid by dipping his head and turning aside and clearing his throat.

Wingate inhaled audibly. "Look, I'm talking about now. Right now. There's been a brutal killing in my county. We have the murderer in custody, and the case against him is dead-on. O'Brien killed that woman. We'll prove it in court, and he'll get the death penalty."

My father stiffened. "Every bit of your evidence is circumstantial. Has the state crime lab confirmed that any of the so-called evidence you took from Jack's place is linked to the crime?"

"The lab report isn't back yet. But I'm sure it will connect the evidence to the crime. Besides," he squinted at my father, "if the evidence is so flimsy, why did Haskin MacHall leave the case?"

"I'm sure he has his reasons."

"Like O'Brien's history of violent behavior."

"You mean that scuffle between two teenage boys?"

Wingate snorted. "He nearly killed the victim. Anyway, it seems that scuffle was enough for Haskin to wash his hands."

"We have new counsel for Jack."

"You mean old Oscar? Too little, too late." He smiled at his own wit. No one else did.

"We'll see."

"You do that, Mr. Wade. You do that. But it seems such a waste of your time. Don't you think?"

My father looked into his paper cup then poured the last of the beer out onto the grass where it pooled and sank. He didn't respond to Wingate. A patch of smoke drifted by. Both men blinked.

"Surely, you know the truth," said Wingate. "The man did it. He killed the teacher—beat her to death. I don't know of your ties to O'Brien, but in spite of that, you have to know the circle will soon be complete, and we will have a lock on his guilt."

The noise continued around us, and the space between my father and Wingate grew into a solid.

"The tie I have with Jack O'Brien," my father said, "is based on one man believing in another. Unfortunately for you, Mr. Wingate, your job is always to condemn. Isn't it?" My father raised his eyebrows slightly. "It must be so dark where you are, where you aren't allowed to look into the heart of a man."

Wingate's face reddened. "You'd better be damn glad I do my job—that someone is willing to challenge that darkness, as you put it."

My father smiled.

"You've lived in Baker City how long?" asked Wingate. "Less than a year if I'm correct."

"That's right."

"So, you're really an outsider. Aren't you? Best you step back and let folks with lifelong roots handle this. We won't coddle mad dogs."

At that precise moment, a woeful howl and static filled the air. Someone tapped a microphone and said "testing" three times. The district attorney looked toward the stage then back at my father, nodded to Lazarus McKay, and moved away. They watched Wingate until he dissolved into the crowd. My father crushed his paper cup and threw it toward a garbage can—he missed.

An overweight, red-faced man wearing an orange cowboy shirt and a dark brown Stetson called for attention. He *howdied* real loud and introduced a gray-haired man who'd come all the way from New York. In a deep voice, the man lauded the exploits of the first cattle ranchers in the valley with tales of hardship and tough men. As the speaking went on, my father and I sauntered back and got some berry pie and stood quietly until the dedicating was over. When the canvas shroud was slipped from a stone pillar in the center of the park, the applause was strong and respectful. I didn't understand what all the fuss was about, but whatever it was, the people there were serious about it. Later, I went over to the monument and ran my hands over the letters chiseled into the gray granite. At the top it read *In Memory of the American Cowboy*. In between there was lots of words about great cattle drives and men of courage. It was dated for that very day: *Dedicated August 9, 1948*. The stone was cool, and the edges of the words new and sharp. Surely, it would last forever.

≋☆

My father's face was taut when we walked back to the McKay tables to find my mother. He'd tightened up from the moment he met up with Haskin MacHall. Then the go-round with T.C. Wingate, I'd never been around when grown men were on anger's edge. It had made me shaky.

My mother rose from the conversation she was having with two women when she caught sight of my father. She excused herself and came to him, steering him away from the tables and stood close while he spoke emphatically, slicing the air with the edge of his hand. She gently rubbed a hand across his back and listened until he got it all out. I drifted closer.

"Why are you surprised?" I heard her say. "Ken. Look at me. You took this stand. If you're going to dish it out, you've got to take it." She delivered her opinions in a nodding motion. "Right? Am I right?"

He stood with his hands on his hips and nodded back to her. He gave her a kiss on the cheek, and they returned to the tables.

Lazarus McKay was waiting and met my father with a smile.

"Well, Ken, how you holding up? That was a little awkward, there, with Wingate."

My father slid his hands into his back pockets and looked at the ground. "Yeah. It was that."

"You acquitted yourself very well, I thought. Had Terhune back on his heels. Never hurts to know the competition up close, I say.

In fact," said McKay, waggling a forefinger, "I'm not so sure that he thinks his case is near as strong as he puts on. What was your impression?"

My father merely shrugged. Maybe he found some solace in McKay's observations; I don't know. Anyway, it was hard to tell; every day was different for my father when it came to Jack O'Brien: Could be up on a Monday and down by Wednesday.

-15-

My father didn't have to wait until Wednesday. It was *down* the very next day. Both of Jack O'Brien's wrists were wrapped with adhesive tape when he was led in to meet his new lawyer. The suicide attempt had happened in the early morning hours. Jack O'Brien had used the edge of a soup spoon he had sharpened on the concrete wall of his cell.

By early afternoon, Herb Gaskill was reporting on KBKR that the accused in the Dugan killing had attempted to take his own life and that there had been a change in attorneys. The next day's *Democrat-Herald* would have a story on page one with Oscar Doolittle's picture alongside one of T.C. Wingate with a headline clear across the top of the front page: **Accused in Dugan Killing Attempts Suicide.** Beneath that: **New Attorney Appointed.**

Jack O'Brien trying to take his life staggered my father. He had rushed down to the jail, but they weren't letting anyone visit but Jack's attorney. That evening, my father picked at his food and wandered about the house aimlessly before disappearing outdoors; he was gone for a long time.

By the time he came back, I had screwed up my nerve to ask him to tell me more about Warney Webster. He was standing at his humidor, dipping a curved stem pipe and thumbing tobacco into it. When he drew the flame into the bowl, I said, "Tell me about Warney."

He squinted at me.

"You already know about that," he said. I could smell beer on his breath.

"Yeah, but I was wondering...what was he like?"

My father pulled the pipe from his mouth and looked at it, reflecting. Smoke sifted out through his lips. "Warney loved life," he said. His eyes were looking but not seeing. "He could be a little wild, but he was a good kid."

"If he liked living why'd he...do that...what he did?"

My father looked down at me with a quick turn of his head. I inhaled and took in the smell of burley tobacco along with it.

"He was scared, Philip. More scared than he'd ever been in his life. He wasn't laughing. There wasn't anything funny anymore. Locked in a cage, people threatening him, accused of something he didn't do."

"Like Jack O'Brien?"

"Yeah, like that." He struck another match. "Just like that."

"But Jack O'Brien didn't die," I said.

My father stared off at the wall. "No, thankfully, he didn't," he said, his voice dropping to a whisper.

"He must have been scared, though," I said. "Really scared."

My father's jaw muscles clenched, and the pipe stem snapped like a carrot stick in his grip. He held the pieces out and gently set them in the ashtray by the humidor and brushed his palms together.

"Time for bed, son." He patted me on the back and pushed me along toward my bedroom. He stayed up awhile after that. I could smell more tobacco smoke.

Oscar Doolittle came by the house to assure my father that Jack O'Brien was okay. My father had wanted to bolt down to the jail again and get in Jack's face. Oscar calmed him and got a promise that he wouldn't go to see Jack for a spell: *Give him a chance to get his face back, Ken, swallow his shame. You can't see him now anyway.*

Right then, I was moved to write another letter to Jack. I'd planned on writing him once a week after that first one, but I never did. Not until that day. I couldn't imagine someone cutting himself on purpose. I had different pictures in my head of what that might look like, actually slicing my skin and seeing blood come out. Jack must be mighty low, and I figured maybe he'd like getting another letter from me. So I took my school tablet to the kitchen table, and I wrote on the pale blue lines—to the man in the cell.

Dear Jack O'Brien,

  I'm sorry that you cut yourself. Did you do it because you're you sad about being in that jail? I would be. My dad's friend hanged himself in jail a long time ago. He was scared my dad said. Don't do that Jack. I am sorry that your dad died in that wreck, too.

                        Your friend,
                        Philip Wade

I found an envelope in the kitchen drawer and, in a moment of distraction, gave it to Oscar Doolittle to deliver. He said he would and patted me on the shoulder while he and my father were discussing something about the legal hurdles ahead of them. The uproar came later.

With Oscar Doolittle's assurance that Jack O'Brien would recover from his wounds and wouldn't be so stupid again, my father bounced back and regained an edge for the struggle ahead. And none too soon, because his name was once again in the newspaper as the person who'd arranged new legal counsel for Jack O'Brien. The Wades became a renewed target. It was open season on our family, and mostly on my father.

For the first couple of days, it was like the first siege. David and I were still forbidden to answer the phone, but that didn't keep me from racing to the living room with every call. I would stand wide-eyed as my mother answered and wait to see if she would hang up without speaking or not. After two or three nasty calls, my mother took the receiver off the hook and put a pillow over it so we didn't have to hear the hum on the line. A few days later, she took the pillow away, and that was it. The rabid telephone callers may have given up, but the news hounds, as my father called them, were still in a state of agitation.

Since my father wouldn't give out statements over the phone, a reporter from the *Democrat-Herald* came out to house. My father met the guy at the front door and backed him out onto the porch. He was skinny and wore a rumpled tweed jacket. He wanted a statement from my father about the change in attorneys—didn't that seem to weaken Jack O'Brien's case? *No comment,* was my father's response, as instructed by Oscar Doolittle. Herb Gaskill called from the radio station. "Mr. Wade," my father imitated Gaskill's radio voice, "Mr. Wade, a number of observers feel that, while Mr. Doolittle is a fine old gent, there's a big disparity between his skills and influence and those of Haskin MacHall. Don't you think the loss of MacHall lessens O'Brien's chances when the case goes to trial?"

Again, no comment from Kenneth Wade.

The climate did a turnabout at the funeral home too. Arthur Woodhull had received some calls from the irate fringe and from the press. In addition, a group of his business associates and golfing cronies were waggling their fingers about my father's involvement with the O'Brien case. Mr. Woodhull finally let my father know that he hoped the matter would be wrapped up soon. The warning was clear.

≋✿

Over the summer, the change in my father was unmistakable. He had become more serious; he laughed less and spent more time in silence at the dinner table. Increasingly, I would find him sitting quietly in the living room, often in the dark, looking at nothing or writing in his ledger. He wasn't a hunter or fisherman or big sports fan, but he would always go out in the yard and play catch with David and me if we asked. He quit doing that, begging off with a gentle pat on my arm and a soft, distracted smile.

I felt a change in myself, too, in fact our whole family changed, all because of Jack O'Brien. Each night, at my bedroom listening post, I heard conversations between my parents that became more and more troubling. After the second barrage of phone calls began, my mother pleaded with my father to drop back and take a less active role.

"Oscar is the attorney," she said. "Let go. Let him do his job."

My father was a warrior. He wasn't a physical man or a strong man, but he had picked up the gauntlet, as I heard Uncle Chet say once during this time. He was going to see this thing through, and he couldn't let go. To my mother's urgings he would simply say, "Margaret, it makes no difference if I never saw Jack O'Brien again—or never mentioned his name—I'm part of this thing until it's over."

I was washing the supper dishes with a pessimist's enthusiasm a few days after the latest newspaper article and a new surge of phone calls, when I heard the engine—the throaty exhaust of the Power Wagon. My hands still dripping, I burst through the screen door and rushed outside, eager to watch another assault on Reservoir Hill. To my dismay, I saw the powerful vehicle roar off of Highway 30, bounce over the sidewalk in front of 1440, and, with the throttle wide open, charge across our measly little yard, all four wheels churning. The sod flew. I couldn't move. When the truck veered past me, I could see into the cab. The anonymous face now had features: Big and wide, eyes bright and glaring, lips pulled back, mouth moving as words were forced out angrily, but muted by the engine noise. Large hands gripped the steering wheel, wrenching and twisting as the beast swerved past me so closely that I could hear the rage escaping—a bellow with no clarity, no defining statement. Just a hateful sound.

The driver continued through our yard and out onto the gravel surface of Eldon Avenue. Still under full power, he cranked the wheel back toward the highway and sent a shower of pebbles and rock into the yard. In slow motion, I saw a stone rise up in an arc and sail over my head toward the house. With the shattering of a window, the brutish vehicle hit the highway asphalt and roared off away from town as it had the other times. I chased after it and, as I ran, heard my own voice screaming, but it seemed from another person. When I got to the corner, the Power Wagon was only an outline. My hero had turned into my enemy.

On a porch down the street, a woman stood watching. I saw her raise a hand to her mouth, but she didn't call out or come toward me. My father was calling my name, and then his hands were on my shoulders, and he turned me toward him. I saw the fear in his face, and I felt his arms around me. We walked back to the house hand in hand to find David and my mother standing in the yard. David was kicking at torn up chunks of grass. My parents looked at one another and at the mess made of our yard. My father nodded to my mother and walked off into the house and called the police.

The Baker City Police Department had only one patrol car, and it happened to be covering an accident at the time of my father's call, so a short time later an officer showed up driving an older blue Pontiac that must have been his personal car. He appeared to be one of the veterans on the force, moving slowly like he had done things a hundred times. His protruding stomach threatened the buttons on his shirt, and a dead cigarette hung out of one corner of his mouth—even when he talked.

He kind of rolled when he walked and approached my father like he had sore feet. "Mr. Wade?"

My father nodded.

"I'm Sergeant Hacker. Responding to your call."

"Sergeant." The two men shook hands.

The policeman held his note pad out in front of him and thumbed off pages until he came to a clean one. "So," he said looking down at the condition of our lawn, "what happened here? Looks like you had a visitor." He tried to laugh but ended up coughing.

"I didn't see it myself, but my son, Philip, did."

He looked over at me kind of sideways and pulled a pencil out of his shirt pocket. "That right, Sonny? You saw this happen?"

I nodded and started to rattle off what I'd seen.

"Whoa, now," he said. "Let me get a few details down first." He drew in a breath you could hear really clear, looked at the house, and pushed his billed cap back on his head. "What's the address here, again?" he asked, moistening the pencil tip in his mouth.

For the next few minutes, he wrote down everything about us: Our address, our phone number, all of our names, about what time the incident occurred, and a bunch of other stuff. Afterward, he pulled a Zippo lighter out of his pocket and lit the dead cigarette in his mouth, took a drag, and coughed. He pulled up on his pants with one hand, holding his note pad in the other. Finally, he looked over at me.

"Now, then, Sonny…"

"Philip," my father said calmly. "His name is Philip."

The officer raised his eyebrows and nodded. "Sure, Philip. Okay, Philip, what did you see?"

I told him everything. Guess I was pretty animated, because every now and again he would pat the air with his hand and slow me down. But he wrote it all down as far as I could tell. When he was done, he flipped his note pad closed, stuffed it into his back pocket, and wandered around looking at the ruts in our yard. David and I were right behind him all the time. He would chuckle when he turned and found us tracking his every move. Finally, he came back to where my parents stood. My father had waited patiently, arms folded across his chest. My mother stood back, still wearing her apron, and watched.

The policeman rubbed his chin and shook his head. "Well, sure made a mess outa your yard. Does the boy's description of the vehicle remind you of anyone you know?"

My father shook his head.

"Umm. You haven't had a run in with anyone lately—I mean anyone who might have a grudge?"

My father looked at the officer for a moment, then unfolded his arms.

"Sergeant Hacker, we've been getting angry phone calls for the better part of a week. I think this incident is just more of the same."

The officer looked my father knowingly. He took off his cap, scratched his thinning hair, and tugged the cap back into place and said, "Maybe I have some ideas about this. Let me look into it and get back to you."

The two men studied each other some more. "I'd appreciate that," was all my father said.

With that, Sergeant Hacker touched the brim of his cap to my mother and waddled back to his car. Two days later, my father received a phone call from Hacker. He had located the owner of the vehicle, a man the name of Lenny Paris who had a place out on Schaffner Creek Road, outside of Baker City limits. If my father wanted to press charges, he would have to bring the county sheriff in on it. Hacker assured my father that he had taken Paris to task. The fellow was repentant—and anxious to avoid being arrested. I think that my father let Sergeant Hacker pull the "good old boy" routine on him, rather than take the matter further—if Paris stayed clear of our family and paid for the damage to our yard and the broken window. That was the agreement.

One day a short time later, a little man in a black Chevrolet pickup showed up unannounced and repaired our damaged lawn. He brought in fresh loam to fill the ruts, rolled it, and reseeded. He came every morning for most of a week and watered until the seed took hold. David and I never knew who he was, and my parents told us to stay clear of him. About the same time, someone from Derry Paint and Window called and made an appointment to repair the window.

≋✧

The following Saturday afternoon, Reverend Hewett dropped by with a sack of ripe tomatoes from his garden. He and my father sat out on the front porch steps, elbows on their knees, watching the world flow by on Elm Street. I figured they wouldn't be talking about tomatoes, that the conversation would hinge on some really good stuff, but only if I could listen but not be seen. I leaned up against the house around the corner, close enough to hear. I had my baseball mitt so I could start popping the ball into it if I was discovered. John Hewett was a bit too cheery. He talked fervently about his garden and his bumper crop of tomatoes and corn and zucchini squash. I listened to the idle talk, fingered my mitt, and waited for him to bring up the real reason for his visit.

At some point, Reverend Hewett ran out of garden exploits and simply quit talking. Evidently my father had nothing to add because it got real quiet. I was about to peek around the corner when John Hewett cleared his throat and got to the point.

"Missing you at church," he said easily.

My father answered in shorthand. "Been on call."

"I see. Got you doing that mighty regular, huh?"

"Seems so."

"Must put a strain on family life."

"Oh, we manage."

"And church?"

"Well…I'm taking sort of a leave of absence from church right now."

"Really. Sorry to hear that. Hate to see you missing the spiritual side of your life."

It got quiet again. I could visualize my father's jaw muscles clenching and unclenching. I am pretty certain he wasn't in any mood to be faulted. At least that's how I could tell I was in trouble.

As soon as those jaw muscles tightened up, I knew to revise my behavior. The reverend wasn't privy to that insight.

There was a pause before my father responded. "Right now, John, your church is one of the last places I want to be. Frankly, I would get more compassion and fairness from the boys over at the Red Leaf Tavern."

"That's severe. You know, Ken, there are some mighty fine folks in our church and this town. Mighty fine."

"I know that."

"And not everyone's against you."

"That right? Wouldn't know."

"I'm truly sorry, Ken. But have you thought that maybe it's time for you to drop this thing and let the law run its course?" When my father didn't respond, Reverend Hewett said, "Ken, sometimes a man can only do so much."

It was quiet for a moment then my father said, "Thanks for the tomatoes."

John Hewett uttered a stunned good-bye and left my father sitting on the porch. I slipped away with my baseball and glove and wondered if things would ever be the same again.

As they did before, the phone calls tapered off after a week. Without comment, my mother used Reverend Hewett's tomatoes in salads and sandwiches. She wasn't one to waste perfectly good food, especially fresh, vine-ripened tomatoes.

-16-

The next week, my father went to visit Jack O'Brien for the first time since he'd cut himself and discovered my second letter, the one that Oscar Doolittle had hand delivered for me.

I came running in from outdoors that day, just after my father had gotten home from visiting the jail, eager to hear the latest about Jack O'Brien. Instead, I ran headlong into my father's hardened face, dark from the flush he was still carrying. He was cursing, but my mother was not trying to stop him. He spun around when he heard me come in the back door.

"Philip! This." He flapped the tablet paper with my writing on it. I froze. "You wrote this. Do you know what you've done? Do you?" I stood rock still. "Damn it, Philip. We had a rule. No letters to Jack unless we saw them first." The outburst appeared to have bled off the heat of his anger. He slumped onto a kitchen chair and looked at my letter and shook his head.

"These things you wrote." His voice was calmer. "What can I say? Jack was upset by what you said. It hurt him greatly. I...I don't know."

"Ken, I'm sure Philip only meant to..." my mother began.

My father waved her off. "It doesn't matter, Margaret. Intentions be hanged. I mean, for crying out loud. Look at this. It's all in here everything to *not* put in a letter to Jack O'Brien. Look at this: That he cut himself, Warney hanging himself, his dad's death. Jesus, mother, and Mary."

My mother looked at me. "He must have known it was a child's way of reaching out to him."

My father shook his head again. "It's not about this," he shook the letter.

"It's about trust. Jack was pacing, beside himself that if a boy knows these things everybody in town must. That he, well, that he will seem more guilty."

"Fine time to think about that," my mother said.

The Kelvinator cracked on and hummed, and there we were, quiet with nothing more to say. My punishment was to eat alone and go to bed early. Later, after David had gone to bed and was asleep, my mother came in and lay down beside me and held my head against her breast and stroked my hair. Some time after that, much later, I awakened to see my father looking down at me. He smelled of tobacco when he leaned down and pulled my covers up and patted me on the head.

That was the end of it. Nothing more was said. I wrote no more letters to Jack O'Brien.

≋✻

Things began to change for the Wades. Maybe it was the shocking attack of the Dodge Power Wagon or the policeman in our front yard, I'm not sure, but some who had remained quiet began to come forward. One was a neighbor two houses down, a man we only knew by sight; he was a mechanic for Clark Motor Company, the local Ford dealer—we knew that much.

One evening the last week of August, while my father watered our newly sprouting grass with a spray nozzle, the mechanic wandered over, giving a wide berth to the young shoots. My father kept watering. The man was wiry, a bit shorter than my father, and a few years older with a shock of black hair and a slightly crooked nose.

"Evening," he said. He wore a light blue work shirt with the sleeves rolled up to his elbows. His forearms were lean and muscled.

My father nodded and said *Evening* back.

"Comin' right along," the man said.

"Uh huh," my father acknowledged.

My father twisted the nozzle down and sent a stream of water out to the edge of the new growth. The neighbor man watched and pulled a stubby, blackened pipe from his shirt pocket, took a leather pouch from his back pocket, and thumbed tobacco down tight into the bowl. He lit it with a kitchen match, and a cloud of white smoke floated out lazily into the evening air, sweet but pungent. I liked it.

"Saw you had a bit of trouble," the man said. His voice was kind of scratchy sounding.

"Yes, a bit."

The mechanic took another puff on his pipe and studied my father for a moment. "Mr. Wade, I'm Harland Foster, a couple of houses down," he said, turning his shoulders slightly in that direction.

My father twisted the nozzle off. "Ken Wade." He extended a damp hand.

Foster reached out with a thick workman's hand. "Nice to meet you. Too bad about all of this," he said looking down at the new grass. "Some people are just plain crazy."

My father grunted a laugh. "Yes, we're finding that out."

"How long have you folks lived here now?"

My father squinted in thought. "I guess a little over eight months."

Foster looked back toward his house. "You know, didn't take a minute to walk over here, but in all that time I haven't come by to welcome you to the neighborhood. Remember when you moved in. Seen you put that new roof on. And," he said looking at me, "I seen you runnin' your lemonade stand. But it takes this here god-awful incident for me to get off my behind and come on over here."

My father's face remained expressionless. "Well, I'll tell you," he said, wiping his hands on his pants, "it's been hell. The family, we've literally been under attack."

Foster drew another puff from his pipe. "Since all this has came out," he said, "hasn't been more than a couple of days go by that Annie and me haven't talked about how you folks come to be tangled up in this awful business." Foster looked at his pipe, it had gone out. He knocked the ashes out and put it back in his shirt pocket. "You really think this here O'Brien is innocent?"

My father didn't say anything.

"I mean, it really seems like the D. A. has the goods on him." Foster looked down and moved a little clod of dirt with a toe of his shoe. "Of course," he said looking up again, "I don't know him like you do."

"He's innocent," my father said, clipped and flat like.

Foster nodded several times. "Well," he said, his voice rose, "when I told Annie that I was a coming over here, she wasn't sure I should. I told her I need to get the man's view on this thing." He looked right into my father's eyes. "And decide how I feel about this neighbor I've never met. And if he's menace or not."

"A menace?" My father's eyes opened wider, and a smile played at the corners of his mouth.

"Darn right." Foster swiveled his head a bit. "This neighborhood's where we live, Annie and me. I got to know about folks living around here. Do I trust 'em? Can we count on one another? And...well...like that." He stopped, and I could see that his neck had gotten red just above his shirt collar.

"So what do you think?" My father held his arms out and looked down at himself. "You think I'm a threat?"

Harland Foster shook his head. "No. I Don't. And I'm sorry as hell for the grief you folks been a taking over this thing. I hear about it. People talk across the yard, in the store, and the like—you know."

My father nodded.

"Well, Ken Wade, I wish you well." Foster stuck out his scuffed hand one more time. "And Mr. O'Brien—I hope his innocence is proved real soon."

With that, the two men gave each other a wave, and Harland Foster walked the less-than-a-minute distance back to his house. From that moment on, whenever Mr. Foster drove by in his pickup he'd toot the horn and wave out the window.

≋✵

While our family life that year was starkly defined by Jack O'Brien, the fact is I only saw the man three times in my whole life. And yet, a day didn't go by that summer without me thinking of or hearing about him. David and I played around and behaved like any kids do at that age, but it wasn't the same. Some kids in the neighborhood didn't come around. I think their parents kept them away. There were a handful of obnoxious ones, like Jimmy Purdue. He would ride by on his bike and yell stuff about killers and other taunting crap. While Jack O'Brien was in jail, our lives settled into a routine that depended on family endurance. Without a lot of talk about it, we grew closer; David and I did our chores with less fuss, my mother was more huggy with her boys, and my father never let a night go by without coming into our bedroom and sitting on our beds before telling us goodnight.

-17-

I guess I thought summer would never end that year. The dis-
agreeable weeks of July and August had blurred into one
long troubled weekend. I was shocked when my mother marched
David and me downtown to endure the torture of shopping for
school clothes. Of course, there were signs that summer was running out. The days were cooler, and back-to-school ads had blos-
somed in the newspaper, but none of that registered until it was
too late. Suddenly, it hit me, and a butterfly chill curdled in my
stomach. Summer was going, going, gone, and I would soon be
strapped to a desk again, inside looking out.

Usually, I was eager to go downtown. Main Street spread so big
and wide with buildings so imposing. Hotel Baker—its art deco
presence towering ten stories high—was the tallest building in all
of Eastern Oregon. I thought that this Art Deco must be a very
rich man to own such a mammoth building.

Memories of wandering the aisles of the huge Bashe-Sage
Hardware Company, with its pungent smells and gleaming sights
linger still along with my many trips to the Carnegie library built
of native gray tuff stone. Smelling the books, selecting a volume
from the shelf, spreading its pages, and taking up the words print-

ed there—that experience first reached inside me in that place.

However, on that day, I was not feeling reverent. The sting of shopping for my own judgment day had been an unfair trick. The afternoon was dismal, as was the thought of a disappearing summer. My mother thought I was unappreciative of new clothes that had cost precious dollars.

The reprieve from my gloom came when Pearl Dorsey appeared at our front door shortly after we had returned from shopping for prison clothes. She stood loose and alive in the doorway.

"Hi, Philip," she said, her hands jammed into the pockets of her jeans, a wide smile displaying those white teeth of hers.

My mother appeared at the door holding one of my new shirts. "Hello, Pearl."

"Hi, Missus Wade."

"Been down buying school clothes. Boys just keep growing. Can't keep up.

You all ready for school?"

Pearl shrugged. "Yeah, I guess. Summer's about over. Out of my Levi's and back to the old classroom."

My mother smiled benignly. "Something we can do for you?"

"Oh," Pearl smiled at me, "I was just going by and wondered if Philip wanted to walk down to Freddie's and get a Popsicle? My treat," she said.

My mother gave in to Pearl's invitation but dug into her purse and gave me my own dime. Pearl and I moseyed down Elm Street like summer was still in front of us and stood over the ice cream freezer at Freddie Patterson's grocery, the cold creating a fog of white air when we opened the lid. I dug out an orange, Pearl chose banana, then we sauntered off into the warm afternoon licking frozen sugar water. At some point, she looked up at the hill and asked me if I had ever been in the old tunnel.

"Sure, I go there all the time. You want to go? I'll take you," I said. "Right now."

She looked up at the hill. "Okay," she smiled. "One last summer excursion."

Elated, I led the way across the highway, and we scrambled up the hillside into the shallow channel that led into the tunnel. She easily reached the top before me, laughing and brushing the dust off her pants. We stopped outside to catch our breath, grinning and gulping. Cool air came out of the dark mouth and met us with the flat smell of exposed earth and old timbers.

Before going in, we finished off our dripping Popsicles. When I tossed away the little wooden sticks, Pearl was looking at me. "Philip," she said, "I've been wanting to say I'm sorry for what I said about your dad. You know, about that man, Jack O'Brien."

My heart gave a couple of extra beats. I couldn't ever hold anything against Pearl. "That's okay," I said.

She picked up a small rock and tossed it out a few feet. "No, it isn't. Your father wouldn't be standing up for the guy if he didn't believe in him." She looked up and opened her eyes a little wider.

"I said it's okay, Pearl. Let's go."

I ran a few feet into the tunnel and felt the cool air wrap around me and enter my lungs. She followed and all sound from outside was replaced by the muffled plodding of our feet in the powdered dirt of the tunnel floor. It was great, being alone with Pearl in that dark, special place. But when I looked back at her in the dim light, I saw a human silhouette appear beyond her at the tunnel entrance. Then another. I blinked and a bad feeling rushed into my chest.

"Pearl," I whispered. "Look."

She turned and stared, bending over, then she went down on one knee. For a long moment, no one moved or said anything. Then, the two dark forms began to move into the tunnel, bending over after a few feet. Pearl stayed still and quiet. I stood behind her, my stomach rolling. A dull male voice came out of one of the dark figures.

"Well, well, what we got here?"

The other figure chuckled. "Is that you, Pearl?" It was not a nice laugh.

Pearl stayed knelt down on one knee and didn't say anything.

"I thought that was you I seen climbing up from the road. Looked like your nice little butt from behind."

"Yeah," the other voice spoke again. "And we was just wonderin', now why would Pearl Dorsey be going up to the tunnel with that little squirt kid?"

Little kid? I was destroyed. And I was scared.

"You getting desperate for some manly attention, Pearly?"

"I know that's you, Frank," Pearl spoke out, "and you too, Presley Purdue. What're you two up to?"

Both men cackled in the dark. "Just comed up here to help a lady in distress," said one of them.

"I'm not in distress." Pearl repositioned herself onto both knees.

"We say you is. Right, Prez? Swore we heard a call for help from you, Pearly."

"Sure did."

As they spoke, they were moving closer until their black outlines began to take on features. The family resemblance was clear. They looked a lot like their little brother, Jimmy Purdue, only bigger and meaner. Their eyes were wide, adjusting to the dark, and they each had cold grins on their faces, revealing big piano key teeth—the Purdue trademark. They stopped a few feet away and squatted down, blocking the way back. I could hear their breathing, and the smell of them came over us—a musky body smell mixed with smoker's breath.

"So now, missy," said Frank, "just how can we help you?"

Presley Purdue bounced on his haunches and kept looking at Pearl. His mouth hung open in a gaping grin.

"I don't need any help." said Pearl. "And you know it."

I was so scared, my throat was practically closed up. I was locked in place, and there wasn't a trace of spit in my mouth.

"Now, we say you do need help," said Frank Purdue. The one called Presley belched.

"You've been drinking," Pearl said.

"So what? It's a hot day," said Frank Purdue. "Now, I think you want this here kid to get on outa here so we can make sure you is helped all proper like. Am I right, Pearl?"

"You can't do this," she said. "Are you crazy? Or just stupid?"

Neither man spoke. All I heard was their ragged mouth breathing.

"You want him to get hurt? 'Cause that's what'll happen, us being so stupid an all."

Still on her knees, Pearl looked back over her shoulder at me. She smiled a strained smile. "Philip," she said real soft. "Philip, go on back. Okay?"

I shook my head hard once. "No." My voice, barely audible, cracked.

She looked down, then back at the Purdue brothers. I could see her shoulders rise and fall, her breathing tense and shallow.

"Pearl." The voice from Frank Purdue was hard.

"Philip, go on," she said. "I'll be all right. I know these guys. They're just talking tough—they won't do anything."

"That's right, kid," squawked Presley Purdue. "We's real good friends of Pearly. You just run on home to your killer loving papa. Yeah, we know who you are, you and that stupid old man of yours. Jesus, what a fool."

They knew who I was. I was shaking so bad, I couldn't have moved right then anyway. "No he isn't," I said, my voice cracking again. "He knows Jack O'Brien is innocent."

"Mouthy kid, just like his dimwit dad," said Frank. "Look squirt, you get on outa here."

"Pearl," I said with a little more force, "I'm not leaving you."

She reached out and touched me on the arm then squeezed it. "Please go, Philip. It's okay." She tried to sound perky, but her voice caught in her throat.

"Yeah, kid, get your butt out of here. Now." Frank Purdue raised up in a threatening manner.

I knew Pearl was trying to protect me, and I wanted to protect her, but I couldn't. I decided to act like I was leaving and started to move out of the tunnel, stopping to touch Pearl on the shoulder. She touched my hand with hers as I passed. As I approached the Purdue brothers, my body shook with fear. They looked at me, and when I started to squeeze by, Presley Purdue clamped my arm in a hurtful grip and shoved me past them. Sour breath, laden with the stink of beer, filled my nostrils when I stumbled by. No one spoke.

My vision swimming, I wobbled to the entrance. When I looked back, I could see the three white faces staring at me out of the dark. My heart was pounding. I was so afraid for Pearl. At first, I staggered away thinking of running for help, but by that time it would be too late. Tears filled my eyes again. I felt so powerless. I grabbed up stones and ran back into the tunnel's mouth. The Purdue brothers had their backs to me now. I threw first one rock and then another as hard as I could. One hit a beam, but the next thunked into a body, and there was a grunt of pain.

"What the hell!" bellowed one of them.

I threw more rocks, some striking home, others missing. I was yelling. I went out to grab more stones and hollered out onto the highway, begging for help. I threw more stones and heard more of them hit those hunkered bodies. I heard them cursing, as they started back toward me. Down on the highway, a farm truck slowed, its flat bed piled high with hay bales, and a man's squinting face peered up at me. I waved and yelled. I could see him so clearly. But he only spat out the window and drove on. When I turned, the Purdues were coming out of the tunnel, blinking through squinting eyes.

They started for me, but Frank Purdue saw the truck and grabbed his brother by the arm. They lurched away, struggling to keep their feet. Presley followed his older brother, holding the small of his back where evidently one of my rocks had struck him. I turned back to the tunnel and saw Pearl stumble out into the sunlight coughing and slapping dust off of her clothes. Her face was drained. She saw me and ran, tripping across the ground between us, and grabbed me in a tight bear hug.

"Philip," she breathed onto the top of my head. "Are you okay?"

I nodded. "I'm...okay...Pearl. Are you?" I was mumbling into her chest as she held me, and I felt the softness of her breasts against my cheek. It was a strange, wonderful sensation.

She knelt down, held me by my arms, and looked into my wide blue eyes.

"Yes. Nothing happened. Thank you, my brave Philip." She hugged me again and held on for a long time. I didn't mind. She took my face in her hands.

"Philip. Listen, you can't say anything about this to your parents—or anyone."

I shook my head. "We gotta get those guys. My dad'll call the cops and get 'em good."

"No!" She shook me hard twice. "Let me handle this. Nothing happened, not really. Besides, it's just our word against theirs. They'll claim they were just goofing around, and we took it wrong. They'll twist it, Philip. They will."

"Did I hit you?" I said, seeing a scratch on one cheek.

She laughed and reached up. "Yeah, you sure did. One of those rocks you threw glanced off a beam and then off me. But that's okay. The ones that hit those guys really made 'em jump."

"I throwed as hard as I could, Pearl."

"You did good, Philip. But you can't say anything, not yet anyway. I'll let you know how things work out."

I agreed to keep quiet.

≈✧

I was still shaking when I got back home from the tunnel. Instead of banging through the back door screen like I usually did, I eased in through the front door and went to my room. The secret I had to protect went with me. For quite awhile, I sat on the edge of the bed while a movie ran in my head of Pearl and me and the Purdue brothers. I wasn't used to having secrets that size, and I couldn't get calmed down.

I don't know how long I sat there, leaning over on my knees, looking at the floor, before I sensed my mother standing in the doorway watching me, one hand in her apron pocket. When I saw her out of the corner of one eye, I quickly reached under my bed, pulled out a Captain Marvel comic, plopped back against my pillow, and opened it.

She stepped into the room and began picking up various items from the floor: Dirty socks, errant toys, inside-out pajamas.

"You and Pearl have a nice time?" She didn't look at me when she spoke—a tactic she used when seeking information.

"Yeah," was all I offered, feigning keen interest in Captain Marvel's muscular exploits.

"What did you do?" She folded David's pajamas and tucked them under his pillow.

"Got a Popsicle."

More picking up and putting away. "Look at your pants, Philip. Where did you get all of that dirt and dust?"

My face grew hot. I kept the comic book close, masking my guilt. "Oh," I was casual, turning another page, "we climbed on the hill."

My eyes wouldn't focus, the cartoon images were a blur of mixed blues, reds and yellows. There was a silence in the room. I prayed and held the caped hero in a death grip. My face flamed— how much more could I stand? My bedroom was airless.

"Well, get up and take off those dirty pants."

That was all she said. I was elated, jumping up and stripping off the pants in great relief. I didn't look at her when she handed me a clean pair of jeans. I pulled them on quickly and laid back down in my stocking feet, taking up the comic again.

She pulled Captain Marvel from my hands and looked down at me. I thought I might explode. Our eyes met, and I knew mine were about to pop out of my head.

"Philip, are you all right?"

All I could do was stare up into her face. What should I say? Nothing. I had promised Pearl.

She put a cool hand on my forehead. "You seem a little warm. Are you feeling okay?"

I put a hand on my stomach. "My stomach doesn't feel too good," I lied.

She sat on the edge of the bed and touched my cheek. "Probably all of that running around in the heat with a Popsicle in you."

Not likely. I could eat three Popsicles, a Baby Ruth bar, and a box of licorice drops, then run nonstop all day and not feel a thing. But I needed an out. So my mother and I played a little game and found one. In the tradition of Captain Marvel, Shazam!

-18-

That evening, after I had picked over dinner, my head still full of what happened in the tunnel, Tom Dorsey called asking if he and Pearl could drop by for a few minutes. A chill surged through me, and by the time they were seated in our living room, my nerves were playing a Sousa march. Of course, my mother delayed things by making ritual coffee and bringing out a platter of Vienna finger cookies.

With my skin crawling, Pearl and I sat there munching cookies and drinking milk while the adults chatted breezily and sipped their coffee. My mother gave David three cookies and sent him outside to play. For once, I would have eagerly joined him. Pearl looked at me a couple of times, smiled weakly, and nibbled on a Vienna finger. Just before I burst into flames, Mr. Dorsey set his coffee cup down and traded in his chit-chat face.

"Well, the sweets are nice, Margaret, but we didn't come for dessert." He turned to look at his daughter for a moment, then at me. I was going to die, my ears were roaring and sweat was forming on my upper lip.

"Something happened today that you should know about." My parents' eyes were glued to Tom Dorsey. They were probably thinking: *What else could happen to our family?*

Dorsey went on. "Pearl and Philip went on a little excursion in the old tunnel this afternoon. You know, up the hill. Anyway, they were followed by the older Purdue bothers, Frank and Presley. They'd been drinking, and it seems that they had intentions on Pearl."

My mother looked at the young girl sitting across from her and slowly brought a hand to her mouth. Their eyes met for a moment, then Pearl reached for her glass of milk. My father looked over at me and back at Tom Dorsey.

"It was getting pretty ugly. The Purdues had Philip and Pearl trapped and forced your son to leave—threatened him, and Pearl." Mr. Dorsey looked at me, his face framed by his jug ears. "But he didn't leave."

My father looked at me again.

"He was foolish. He came back. Thankfully, he was very foolish."

Alarm filled my mother's face. She was remembering finding me in my room and obviously making connections. I couldn't look at her.

"He started throwing rocks and yelling for help. He threw rocks until he drove those two crumbs out of that tunnel, and they slunk away." By this time, Mr. Dorsey was smiling at me, so was Pearl, and my parents were looking at me in amazement. "You have one brave young man there." He leaned forward, elbows on his knees, and looked straight at me. "Thank you, Philip. If you hadn't raised a ruckus, I don't know what would have happened to Pearl."

I was blushing, everyone was smiling at me. I felt like Captain Marvel and an idiot at the same time. I knew that Pearl had saved me from harm, probably more than I had her. When I started to say something, she shook her head. I, Philip Baxter Wade, was the only hero in the room—no cape needed. Shazam!

"So what now?" my father asked, jaw muscles clenching. "Those characters can't get away with that."

"Well," Mr. Dorsey clasped his hands together so tightly his knuckles grew white, "I'll admit, I was furious. Mad enough to confront that whole Purdue clan. But Pearl thought the matter would come down to her and Philip's word against the Purdues. I had her write it all down—you know, what happened and all—and then I called the police."

"What did they say?" my father asked.

"Oh, you know, they'd look into it and asked me to drop Pearl's written account by the station. Then I called Frank Purdue."

"Called him?" My mother was nonplussed. "What on earth for?"

Tom Dorsey sat back and folded his arms. "Oh," he said glancing at my father, "to give him my irate father warning."

My father's voice was flat when he asked, "How'd that go?"

Tom shrugged. "Frank? He started giving me some foul-mouthed lip. Right off. His tuned changed when I told him that I'd informed the police and would be giving them a full written account of their actions. Told him that he and Presley would likely be getting a call from the boys in blue."

"What did he say to that?"

"At first, nothing. Then, when I asked if he understood what I was saying, he just said, 'yeah,' in that dull voice of his. I warned him to leave Pearl and Philip alone. He just hung up."

It was agreed to leave the matter there for the time being. I wallowed in my glory as more coffee, milk and cookies were consumed. The irony in that moment of righteousness is that when the Dorseys were standing on our porch saying their good-byes, out on the sidewalk Velma Lumpkin went by walking her toy Collie dog. She paused and stared up the walk at us, glaring before yanking the leash and literally dragging the poor animal down the street. We all chuckled, and as Velma Lumpkin stomped out of sight, Tom Dorsey turned to my father and commented that he hoped things were going well with the case. Perhaps another changed opinion. It only verified that wherever we were and whatever we were doing, Jack O'Brien was not far behind.

≋✤

Shortly after Tom and Pearl Dorsey left, Oscar Doolittle called and asked if he could drop by for a bit. The last day of August was turning into one to be remembered. By the time Doolittle showed up, my mother had put away the remaining cookies and emptied the coffee pot. She busied herself in the kitchen, not bothering to say hello or offer her usual hospitality with a fresh cup of hot coffee. My mother was forming an intractable stance against the invasion of Jack O'Brien into her family's life. I don't think Mr. Doolittle ever noticed.

He parked his comfortable old Lincoln four-door, a 1940 light green Zephyr, on Eldon Street. My father met him on the front porch where they stood for a few moments in quiet conversation. Something was brewing. They came into the house, and we patiently watched Oscar Doolittle slip out of his suit coat and position himself on the couch. He smiled at me above another bow tie, an awful pea soup green with blue stripes, and blinked his watery eyes—eyes alive with something he evidently couldn't wait to share.

"So?" my father said.

"Like I said, had an interesting day," Oscar Doolittle began in that mellow courtroom voice of his.

"I've been after Wingate for the results of the State Crime Lab's report. You know that."

My father was leaning forward in his overstuffed chair, hands clasped.

"Either he didn't return my calls, or I got the run around that the lab had a big backlog. That can happen, but I wasn't convinced—plus I don't trust T.C. Well," Doolittle grinned, "I have a colleague in Salem, a fellow I worked with years ago in D.C. He agreed to tap his contacts, see if someone would get cozy with the State Police and so on and so on.

"Well," Doolittle wiggled on the couch and rubbed his hands together, "my friend called me today. Guess what?"

My father had a curious smile. "Oscar, I haven't a clue. What?"

"T.C. Wingate has had the state lab's report for two weeks."

I was leaning over the back of my father's big chair, and I could feel him poised like a steel spring. "What were the results?" He looked into Doolittle's smug face. "They didn't connect Jack, did they?"

"No, they didn't!" With that, Doolittle smacked his hands together. My father flopped back in his chair, and the two men just stared at one another, grinning.

"So it's over." My father sat upright. "We can get him out of jail right?"

"No, no. Not yet. For one thing, we aren't supposed to know the results of the report. I can't tip my hand by challenging Wingate with what I know to be true. Might get myself in some trouble and foul up things for Jack."

"So what can you do?" I asked.

Doolittle looked past my father at me. "Well, Philip, we have to be patient. We know that the case against him is specious."

"What's that?"

"Means it looks good, but it isn't true. But we have to force old

163

T.C. to play his hand, to release this exculpatory evidence."

"What's that mean, exculpoo...?"

"Another big word. Sorry, Philip. That means evidence that can clear Jack of any guilt in this case."

"Oscar," my father came in, "have you seen Jack? Did you tell him this yet?"

Doolittle leaned back on the couch. "No. He'd likely start shooting his mouth off for sure—couldn't blame him. But that'd make a mess of things. If Wingate feels cornered by this and senses any threat to his position in this county, he would fight a delaying game. No, we have to maneuver him into a position where finding Jack O'Brien innocent is the right thing to do. We'll help him be an honest public servant by dropping the charges and releasing him."

"How's Jack doing?" my father asked. "I haven't seen him in a spell. Has he healed up?" The matter of my letter wasn't mentioned.

Doolittle pursed his lips. "Jack's doing okay. Not great, but okay. And I think his wrists are okay. But he is one mad hombre. Imagine being penned up and charged with something this heinous, something you absolutely did not do—then switching to an old geezer lawyer in the middle of everything. I don't have a clue if he has any confidence in me or not."

"Oscar, you are great. Jack will learn that soon enough and be very grateful."

With a shrug, Doolittle reached for his briefcase, which he had never opened, and stood up. "Maybe. The main thing for now is that we know we've got old T.C. by the short hairs, right where we want him. I can't wait to squeeze him a bit and get that lab report released—very shortly."

"By the way, Oscar," my father said, "the T. stands for Terhune. He hates it. Might come in handy."

"Terhune." Doolittle said the name, stringing it out. "I like it."

≋✦

That night, the air inside 1440 seemed sweeter. I was a hero, and my father walked around grinning. He even flirted with my mother, kissing her on the neck and lifting her off the floor. She acted out her displeasure, but with a smile and an occasional giggle.

Later that night, I heard muffled laughter coming from behind my parents' closed bedroom door and strange sounds that I did not understand until later.

-19-

Right after Labor Day, David and I trudged up the steps of Tiedemann Elementary School, doomed again to hallways, classrooms, and desks that talked back at us with scarred skins. A previous occupant had cut the initials **P** and **A** into the top of my desk. When bored, I would trace the letters with my finger and dream up names those gashes might stand for. Awaiting me was my fifth grade teacher, Theodore Pragg. He was tall, had a pock-marked face, a mass of black hair, and glasses with very thick lenses. It was kind of eerie when he peered at you with eyes that looked recessed and very small. However, he was a kind man and a good teacher. He had a special way of making me want to do my best. I felt very successful as a student in Mr. Pragg's class that year.

The other thing facing us at Tiedemann that fall was the ghost of Mrs. Dugan. When I stopped in front of her old classroom, wary and curious, I discovered that we'd been tricked. Instead of being a second grade classroom, Katherine Dugan's old room was now a sixth grade class. Mr. Smith, a wide, bald-headed, bear of a man, stood at the door once covered with flowers. Now it was his classroom. He saw us looking in and said, "All right, boys—you, too, Sally—get on to your classrooms, move along." He waved a big arm and swept us away from a harsh memory.

I was curious about who would be taking Mrs. Dugan's place. David was now in the second grade, and I wondered what person would end up teaching Mrs. Dugan's class. That first day, I wandered around until I found the second grade classroom. It was now room 12. The small brass metal frame by the door to the room carried a little card with the name "Miss True" printed on it. I peeked in and saw a woman sitting at the teacher's desk who was younger than Mrs. Dugan had been, but not as pretty or as slender. She had shoulder length brown hair framing a sort of roundish face and wore dark-rimmed glasses. The room was decorated with cheery alphabet cutouts, mounted on bright colored construction paper. A vase of yellow flowers sat on her desk. There was nothing drab about the room. I don't know what I expected, maybe a woman wearing black, very serious looking, and a room breathing gray fog.

While I was taking all of this in, the woman looked up and saw me peering in. She smiled. It was a nice smile, very warm and open. "Hello," she said, still smiling. "Can I help you?"

I just shook my head and walked away. That was all I needed, to see who had been recruited to try and take the place of Mrs. Dugan; Mrs. Dugan who would forever be pretty, petite and remembered as a lovely person who met a tragic end. She would become an heroic figure at Tiedemann and gain in stature as the years went by.

David did end up in Miss True's class. He loved her and didn't remember Mrs. Dugan much, anyway. As much as I hated to see summer end, the fall of 1948 was off to a pretty good start. I was able to enjoy the afterglow of my moment of heroism for quite awhile. It looked as if Jack O'Brien would soon be released and our family as well. David and I each had teachers we liked, so school was not the prison it had been the year before.

-20-

Oscar Doolittle pursued the district attorney diligently for another week with phone calls and attempted personal visits after learning of the state crime lab results. He was a pest, always in Wingate's face, very pointedly asking about the status of the crime lab analysis. The D. A. was either unavailable or insistent that he had not yet received the lab report. Doolittle was enjoying himself. He feigned annoyance and would leave Wingate's office in exaggerated umbrage or hang up abruptly when he wasn't given the answers he wanted.

My father and I were caught up in the old man's escapades. Most every evening that week, we would sit in our living room after supper—sometimes Uncle Chet would be there, too—and listen to Oscar Doolittle recount that day's battle tactics. That's what he called each step he took: *A battle tactic.*

His first tactic was to confront the district attorney straight on to prevent Wingate dodging his inquiries. No matter Doolittle's persistence, he was being taken lightly by the D. A. and his staff, all of whom were having their laughs over his assumed ineptness.

Tactic two: Herb Gaskill at KBKR was surprised when Jack O'Brien's attorney finally agreed to an interview; likewise the

Democrat-Herald reporter who had been pursuing the case. Exactly fourteen days after receiving the news from Salem, Oscar Doolittle was quoted on KBKR's newscasts challenging the Baker County District Attorney to release findings of the state crime lab. The *Democrat-Herald* ran a front page story with pictures of T. C. Wingate and Oscar Doolittle side by side.

O'Brien Attorney Challenges D. A.
Demands Release of Crime Lab Report

Oscar Q. Doolittle, attorney for Jack O'Brien, is calling for the release of the Oregon State Police Crime Lab report regarding the Katherine Dugan murder case. Doolittle has threatened to contact the Oregon State Police Crime Lab, personally, if the district attorney has not responded within 24 hours.

O'Brien, 32, is being held and charged with the murder of Katherine Elaine Dugan, 46, on May 23 of this year. Evidence which the police suspected might connect him to the murder was taken from O'Brien's residence at the time of his arrest in July and forwarded to the crime lab some time after the suspect was taken into custody. The exact date the evidence was submitted is not known.

"My client is entitled to know the results of the crime lab's analysis," said Doolittle. "Even allowing for a backlog in Salem, more than enough time has elapsed for the state's report to have reached the Baker County District Attorney, Mr. Terhune Wingate."

The District Attorney was unavailable for comment. A spokesman from the district attorney's office said that the status of the Oregon State Crime Lab report in the matter of the

Dugan case is uncertain at this time. No indication was given as to when results of the state's analysis would be available.

≋✻

Tactic three: Oscar Doolittle waited for his salvo to bear fruit. The morning after the article in the paper, he went to breakfast with Chet Stillman at the Inland Cafe. They sat in their usual seat near the front door, and each ordered a big breakfast. As usual, the cafe was packed. On this occasion, they did not go unnoticed as just two old coots killing time.

Two things happened: They were either deliberately ignored, or people stopped to say a word and pat Oscar on the back. According to Oscar, the most fuss on the grapevine was that Wingate was furious at the use of his first name in the newspaper and on the radio. He despised the name *Terhune* and had gone to great lengths to keep it private. He went by T. C. even on legal documents. Oscar found that the idea of Wingate in a rage over the use of his own name almost as much fun as bringing him to ground on the lab report.

Of course, it wasn't as important as getting Jack O'Brien out of jail. And, even while Oscar Doolittle enjoyed the news coverage that morning at the Inland Cafe, he still had his eye on the clock. When 24 hours passed, he clearly intended to contact the Oregon State Police and make a lot of noise in town when he did.

It didn't come to that. At 3:00 p.m. that afternoon, T.C. Terhune Wingate called Oscar Doolittle at his house on the ranch. Their conversation was short.

≋✻

Our house was bubbling with excitement that evening. Old 1440 was a palace, Cinderella for one night; her rounded wallpaper corners, her sagging foundation, her awkward plainness were all replaced with a happy heartbeat and an inner elegance. Jack O'Brien was to be a free man by the next day. When my father heard the news from Oscar Doolittle, he decided that there should be a celebration. My mother and Aunt Ruth joined forces to prepare a quick, but hearty, meal. My father splurged on two fresh baked apple pies from Scotch's Bakery, and Oscar Doolittle brought a bottle of red wine.

The oak table had been moved from the kitchen and the extra leaves, inserted. Over the pleasant sounds of breaking bread over my mother's lace table cloth, Uncle Chet rose on his uncertain legs and proposed a toast to Oscar. Everyone raised whatever glass they had. David and I raised our milk glasses. Oscar stood and proposed a toast to my father. My father toasted our mother.And so it went until everyone was toasted—even David and me.

My father rose one more time. "And now I toast Mr. Jack O'Brien for suffering the agony of being wrongly accused and enduring in spite of it."

We all solemnly raised our glasses again. When he sat down, my father looked at the serious faces and smiled broadly.

"Hey, no sour pusses here. We've won!" He looked at Oscar and said, "Okay, Oscar, tell us all of it again. From the moment Terhune called until you saw Jack. Every morsel. And don't leave anything out."

The old man nodded. I thought he looked tired. His white shirt was wrinkled and bow tie askew. But behind the lined face, his eyes were bright, and a smile held his thin lips.

"It has been delicious, you know," he began. "Not for Jack, of course, but on his behalf. I haven't had this much fun in awhile." He looked over at Chet Stillman, whose pugnacious face looked even wider when he grinned. "Nothing makes winning sweeter than having a challenging adversary. That, and having the goods on him when he doesn't know it."

I listened like my teachers wished I would, savoring the story of a victory which, it seemed for a time, might not ever come. Oscar set his elbows on the table and leaned his chin on clasped hands.

"Well, he said, "after all of our maneuvering, I simply went home and waited. I settled into my leather chair and picked out a good book. I had no idea if Wingate would call my hand or if he would blink.

"By mid-afternoon I was beginning to wonder. I had just gotten me a glass of lemonade and settled back down, when the phone rang. It was him." Oscar paused and gripped his bony hands together and looked around at us. "He identified himself—very formal, I must say—and made some official sounding comments about the evidentiary report from the state crime lab. I said a couple of, *I see's*. Then, in a very tight voice, he spit it out. He finally had to say it. He had exculpatory evidence which seemed to exonerate Jack O'Brien in the Dugan case. That he wouldn't be pressing the case against Jack any further."

He paused, and his gentle chuckle vibrated.

"The man even questioned the reliability of their citizen tipster, Mrs. Lumpkin. He flat didn't have a case left. We traded a few more words, then he took a deep breath and said he would be releasing Jack tomorrow morning once the paperwork was completed. And that was it." Oscar shrugged then poured himself another glass of wine.

My father's need for completion floated like a balloon above the table. "What did he say about the evidence? It was all a bunch of baloney, right?"

Oscar nodded. "With great reluctance, Wingate conceded that

none of the evidence they took from Jack's place connected him to the killing. The pieces of cloth matched none of Mrs. Dugan's clothing. Jack had indeed purchased a pane of glass from the lumber yard, explaining the cut on his hand. And none of his tools matched the wounds. Oh, and the blood evidence was also inconclusive since they were both type O-positive."

"I knew it," my father said, "all the time." He leaned back and folded his arms.

"Well," said Uncle Chet, "it didn't work. Oscar taught 'em a thing or two."

"That may be, but I don't think we ought to sit here and gloat," said Aunt Ruth. "There was a murder, remember. The brutal killing of a woman right on the streets of this town. I'm darn glad the authorities did something."

The men's faces dropped like tailgates. The room went awkwardly silent. Aunt Ruth set her jaw and waited. Uncle Chet's broad face tilted toward his wife, his forehead wrinkled in bewilderment.

"Yes, love," he said, "but thinking thataway, I could've been accused of murder. Just think of all the tools in my shop, stuff they could call evidence—it's kinda scary. And think of Jack. Him being locked up all of this time, and being damned-well innocent he was. What if Oscar hadn't stepped up?"

Aunt Ruth's chin jutted out, and she turned an unyielding gaze on her husband.

Oscar Doolittle calmly side-stepped the tension and nodded toward my father. "I got there at the end, Chet, but if it hadn't been for Ken's stance at the beginning, Jack might have easily been indicted and had to stand trial. Who knows what would have happened then? This town wants a conviction for that murder." He sneaked a sideways look at Ruth Stillman.

"No matter," my mother said. "I think Ruth is right." She stared at the remnants of food on her plate, separating cold bits of meat from cold greens with her fork. "The police and district attorney were just doing their jobs—thank heavens." Her face was slightly flushed when she looked at my father. It was just between them now. "Who is Jack O'Brien?" she asked. "What do we know of him, other than that he helped you put a roof on this house—for pay?"

My father clamped his lips down then picked up his juice glass and downed the remaining wine in one swallow.

"No, Ken, you listen." My mother's voice was even, unwavering. "Jack O'Brien could be an ax-murderer in seven states, and you wouldn't know it. Yet you...you charged to his defense as if he were your own brother." She swung a hand out demonstrably. "What if he did it? What if he killed that woman? And what if the particular evidence the police confiscated just didn't have any relationship to the crime? What if the real evidence was buried or... or more likely, thrown in the river?"

"He didn't do it, Margaret." My father's voice was cinched tight, and his jaw muscles flexed a couple of times.

My fork was too heavy to lift from my plate. No one moved or spoke. This was what my mother had been holding in. She had held it in when I asked her to her face. She had held it in when the phone was ringing and ringing. She had held it in when all around us it was *Jack O'Brien, Jack O'Brien*. Now with Jack O'Brien out of danger, she didn't want to hold it in anymore; certainly within this circle of conspirators, she didn't have to.

"Even if he didn't, this entire episode, this...this horrible time, has punished our family. We gave up a big part of our lives for an antisocial hermit of whom we knew nothing."

"Heaven forbid," my father said. "We wouldn't want to put our good old Christian values to the test, now, would we? Hell, it's a much bigger trial to mingle with the faithful at a church potluck. Lots of risk there. Forget someone alone, accused, with no credentials."

My mother smiled. "Come on, Ken. That's not the reason. That's not why you did this," my mother said. "Jack O'Brien was just a catalyst. You picked up the gauntlet and decided to champion this thing. We know why, don't we? And once you got underway, you would not stop. For that, we've paid—the boys and me."

My father looked at David and me. I'm sure we looked uncertain about this tense dialogue between our parents, but I knew my mother was talking about Warney Webster.

"Don't look at the boys, they've heard it all. The time to worry about them was back in July. Since then, we've lost friends, become estranged in our own church, and isolated in this neighborhood." As pointed as her words were, she spoke them softly, almost reverently. "And…we've had to live in almost a hostage environment. I only hope it has all been for the right cause."

The celebratory evening ended quietly; 1440 turned from a glittering carriage back into a pumpkin. Our guests left quietly. Aunt Ruth hugged my mother, while the men looked at the floor. My father smiled appropriately and patted the departing men on their backs. We all waved farewell. Nothing more was said about Jack O'Brien, good or bad. All had been said. What would happen next, would happen. As a family, we cleared the table and washed dishes, without more than a few words spoken.

David and I went to bed in a cocoon of silence, having been hugged and kissed by each of our parents. I laid awake in the dark, and my mind was racing with scenes and words and moods of all that had happened. It churned into a blur until I fell asleep.

-21-

I awoke suddenly. It was still dark, still nighttime, when the knocking came. Someone was at our door. I heard muffled voices and the sound of someone moving about. It was my father. I raised up on an elbow and heard him stumbling in the dark.

"Turn on the light, Margaret, I can't see."

The knocking came again. The lamp on my mother's nightstand glowed on, and my father, wrestling himself into his bathrobe, lurched out into the hallway his face pinched in a scowl. "Who in the devil?" he complained.

I sat up in bed and listened. David slept on. The front door opened with its usual groan, and the vibration of voices rumbled back to my ears. After a few moments, I heard the door close, and a light went on in the living room. The voices continued. It was just too much; I had to know who it was. There was one light on, a table lamp. It cast a yellow wedge of light beneath the shade, illuminating the faces of my father and Jack O'Brien. It took me a moment to recognize him, because his hair was shorter than I remembered, and he looked pale, his robust skin tone had faded. He was hunched over in the platform rocker, leaning on tucked-in elbows when he saw me peering from the hallway. He looked up, and my father followed his eyes.

"Philip," he whispered. "It's okay. Come on, son, over here." He patted the place next to him on the couch.

I approached slowly in my Roy Rogers pajamas. After months of the name and the shadow of Jack O'Brien being ever present, he was sitting in our living room. The man who had become my father's cause and my mother's angst was a breathing presence. I sat on the couch up against my father. Jack O'Brien smiled at me.

"Hello, young fella," he said. His voice had a fogginess to it. "Sorry to wake you."

"That's okay."

My father rubbed his hand through my hair and patted me on the back. "Okay, Jack, what's going on? Oscar told me that Wingate was going to release you in the morning."

Jack O'Brien's smile slid into more of a cynical wrinkle. "That's what I heard, too," he said. "But," he raised his arms out like wings, "about an hour ago, Wingate and one of his assistants woke me, rousted me out, and released me on the spot. Just like that. Very hurry up."

At that moment, my mother appeared wearing her apricot colored bathrobe and stood across from us behind the overstuffed chair. She was not smiling.

"Hello, Mr. O'Brien."

Jack O'Brien stood. "Miz Wade, nice to see you again. Sorry about waking everybody up. It's just that I was let out about half an hour ago…and you folks are the only people I really know in town."

"I understand." She stood straight, wooden.

"Jack was just telling me what happened." My father's expression was clearly appealing to his wife to be indulgent.

"I see. Well, I'll leave you to sort things out then. I'm happy for you, Mr. O'Brien. Philip, are you coming back to bed?"

"I want to stay, Mom." I prayed for my father to back me up. He did.

"That's okay, Margaret. He can stay." Another test of wills.

My mother stiffened even more. "Very well. Goodnight, then, Mr. O'Brien, and all the best to you."

O'Brien rose up part way again. "Thank you, ma'am."

My father looked at his watch. "My god, Jack, it's after midnight. Why on earth would Wingate pull a stunt like this?"

Jack O'Brien shrugged and leaned back in the rocker. "Got me. They woke me up, gave me my clothes, and told me to get changed. Before I knew it, I was out on the street in front of the courthouse."

"And that was it?"

"Well, Wingate did tell me it would be better for all concerned if I got out of town."

"Oh, really?" My father's eyebrows went up.

"Yep. And for good measure, he told me to not be found wandering around the streets tonight, or I'd be right back in jail as a vagrant. He knows I don't have no cash money on me. That's why I had to come here."

"I understand." My father was still puzzling. "I think I have an idea of what's going on here. This is Friday night. If Wingate releases you now and tells you to get out of town, he avoids several things. First, no daylight release with you and your attorney facing the news people. Second, he avoids a head-on confrontation regarding your release and why it's taken so long to declare your innocence. Finally, if you aren't the killer, who is? By releasing you tonight, Wingate buys a whole weekend before the reporters can confront him. I'm sure he will be out of town and unavailable until Monday."

Jack O'Brien's smile faded as my father was unraveling his version of district attorney's motives. Without the camouflage of a smile, the man looked tired, he looked weary, and I sensed a lingering anger beneath it all. But he had to hold it in until he could get clear of Baker City and its D. A. and out of the box he was in. I don't mean to say that as a nine-year-old kid I was wise beyond my years, but I just knew in looking at the man that Jack O'Brien was already gone. He just hadn't left town yet. I looked for the scars on his wrists, but his shirt had long sleeves. My letter suddenly came to mind. I'd thought many times about apologizing, but that would have meant another letter. I studied the drawn face of the man and decided I couldn't do it—not in person.

My father, oblivious to Jack's fatigue, was caught up in the cause—he still wanted to save Jack O'Brien. "You're welcome to stay here for the night," he said. "Tomorrow, we'll get together with Oscar and figure out our next move."

"Ken." O'Brien held up a hand. "Ken, stop. That's enough for tonight, okay? I'm tired, and you guys are losing your sleep time, too. But let me say this," he leaned forward again, his black eyes locked onto my father, "I never had nobody do for me what you done. Not as a kid in trouble. Not in the service. Never. Nobody. Not sure why you come to my defense. Truth is, if things had been reversed, I probably would'na give you a second thought. You didn't owe me a thing. In fact, it's a little weird what you did. But I'll take it and be damned grateful."

With that he leaned back. "Now, can I borrow this couch? I'm pooped."

My father got a blanket for him, and we went back to bed.

There was a strange mood to the house that night. After months of hearing Jack O'Brien this, Jack O'Brien that, to have the real Jack O'Brien sleeping in our living room—it was kind of unreal. Once during the night, I got up to use the bathroom and tiptoed into the living room to see if he really was there. He was. In the subdued light cast from the bathroom, I saw the mound gently rise and fall beneath the blanket and heard a low snorting sound as the real Jack O'Brien breathed in and out—in our house.

The next morning, he was gone. My father arose early only to find the plaid blanket neatly folded on the sofa and no Jack O'Brien. We never saw him or heard from him again. He didn't go back to the shack by the river (it had been boarded up by the city anyway); he wasn't seen anywhere around town after that night. He dematerialized. For the first time since mid-July, Mr. O'Brien was in charge of his own fate.

≅∗

A short time after the papers reported Jack O'Brien's release, his older brother, Dennis O'Brien, drove into town from Fresno and came by our house late one afternoon looking for my father. When my mother told him that he was working, the brother said he was staying down the street at the Oregon Trail Auto Court and wondered if it would be all right if he were to come by that evening around seven. My mother said that she guessed it would all right.

When Jack O'Brien's older brother knocked on our front door that evening, my father was waiting. He let the man in but didn't invite him to sit down or to even move away from the door. My mother, David, and I were there, as well, standing back, curious as to why the man had come to town. Over dinner, my father had grumbled about how shameless it was for Jack's brother to be showing up at this late date.

Dennis O'Brien stood awkwardly, looking first at my father, then at the rest of us. He was much older than Jack, maybe in his fifties. The brothers shared the same dark hair, but Dennis O'Brien's was receding and had lots of gray in it, and where Jack was lean, his brother was heavy and his face carried a jowl.

"What do you want, Mr. O'Brien?" my father asked after an uneasy few moments.

"Uh, well, it's about Jack. I was wondering if you know where he is?"

My father's jaw muscles were flexing. He stared straight into Dennis O'Brien's eyes and said, "No."

O'Brien blinked. "But I thought you…"

"What are you doing here, Mr. O'Brien?"

"I came looking for Jack."

"Why?"

O'Brien inhaled and looked down.. "Okay," he said raising his head, "I let him down, I know that, but I want to make up for it."

"Let him down?" My father snorted. "That what you call it? You didn't let him down, mister. You abandoned him. Let me ask you, would you be here if Jack had been put on trial?"

O'Brien sniffed and looked over at us then back at my father.

"I thought not," my father said. "Good evening, Mr. O'Brien." He reached for the doorknob.

"Look," O'Brien said, "I know that in your eyes I'm a bastard, but can you at least tell me how to find him?"

"I have no idea where he is, and I wouldn't tell you if I did." My father had the door open.

Dennis O'Brien started to leave then turned back. "In any event, thank you for what you did for Jack."

My father looked back at his family. "We didn't do it for you,

---

181

sir. Now please take your shame away from this house."

Dennis O'Brien lowered his head for a moment before stepping out onto the porch. My father shut the door and held onto the knob for a moment before letting go and walking away.

"That's the end of it," he said and went off to read the evening paper.

And it was the end of Jack O'Brien's pull on our family. But it wasn't the end of 1948.

-22-

The *Democrat-Herald* and Herb Gaskill at KBKR had a field day with the release of Jack O'Brien. They took T. C. Wingate to task for having the wrong man in custody for over two months while the real killer remained at large. Of course, that caused another wave of fear and outrage in town, especially among the female population. One evening after supper, David ran inside from playing and announced that that *bad woman* was staring at our house again. My father put aside the paper and stepped out onto the front porch and into a heated glare from Velma Lumpkin. She stood square to the house, her legs set wide apart while holding her little dog by a leash so taut that the dog's front feet were off the ground. My father put his hands in his pockets and looked at the woman but said nothing. David and I were beside him; our mother was in the doorway. The staring contest lasted a minute or so before my father turned and, with his hands on our shoulders, began to herd us back inside the house.

"You let a killer loose!" Velma Lumpkin yelled.

We all turned. My father squinted and clenched his jaw but still didn't say anything. He pushed on us again.

"Hope you're satisfied," the woman yelled. "He does it again, it'll be on your head."

My father closed the door, told us boys to stay inside, and went back to his chair, his pipe and the paper. The mild furor subsided after a few days, and the news folks began focusing on other local issues and the coming presidential election between Dewey and Truman. My father was adamantly against Harry Truman. His moaning over the sitting president and his warnings of dire consequences if he were re-elected, hung in the air at 1440 during those days. The closer we got to November 2nd, the more pronounced were my father's protests or his shouts of joy.

"Margaret, listen to this," he said one evening, carrying the paper into the kitchen after dinner. *"Dewey's lead widens in national poll. He now has an almost unbeatable margin of 44 percent to Truman's 31 percent."* He rattled the paper closed. "We've got him! Truman is as good as gone."

Of course, the lead didn't hold, and in late October my father's buoyancy faded as Dewey began to lose ground. But the journalists and political experts of the day still predicted a smashing victory for Thomas E. Dewey.

On election eve, I remember my father pulling the overstuffed chair in front of the Zenith and camping out there when the returns began to come in. I sat on the floor beneath the radio's green eye and in front of the big speaker and tried to get into the spirit of this national event which was creating such emotion in my father. The numbers soon merged into a glob of indecipherable mush—numbers and babble I didn't understand. About the time my interest would begin to fade, my father would suddenly lean forward.

"Shhh! Wait! Okay, good. That's good." Meaning that Dewey was still leading. Then, he would lean back, nodding and take another cookie off the plate my mother kept full.

If Truman was gaining ground, he would say, "That's all right. It's all right. Harry was expected to do well in those states."

And so it went. Long after David and my mother had gone to bed, weary of it all, I was still sitting up with my father at the radio. The drama for me was in his reactions, the ups and downs—exhilaration one minute, grinding disappointment the next. I didn't know much about Dewey or Truman, but I knew a good show when it came along.

It was in the middle of an election update from the Mutual Radio Network that someone twisted our doorbell. It was after eleven o'clock. My father looked at his wristwatch, grumbled under his breath, and went to see who it was. Words were exchanged at the front door, and a man followed my father into the living room. He looked familiar to me, but I didn't know why at first. His face was pasty and pock-marked, he had sandy colored hair and pouches under his eyes.

"Have a seat," my father said. "This is my son, Philip. We've been listening to the election results. Philip, turn the radio down a bit, would you, son?"

The man sat on the edge of the couch and nodded at me. He rested his elbows on his knees, clasped his hands, and began to slowly massage them.

"So," my father began, "you have a cab company?"

"Yeah, me and my one cab." He laughed and that turned into a cough that he couldn't stop until he had done it three times.

Suddenly, I knew. The Eight-0 Taxi. "We rode in your taxi," I said. "The Eight-0. Dad, he drove us from the train when we first came here."

The man smiled with lips that had no color. "Good memory, young man. I remember that night, too. It was cold, and the moving van was waiting for you."

"Don't remind me," my father said. "So, what's on your mind, mister…?"

"Sorry, Mitchell. Tom Mitchell."

"I'm Ken Wade, and it seems you already know Philip."

Tom Mitchell smiled at me. "Guess so."

My father raised his eyebrows at the man.

"Well," Mr. Mitchell said, "it's about that schoolteacher thing."

"You mean Katherine Dugan?"

"Uh huh. I know you was involved in helping the guy, O'Bryant, was it?"

"O'Brien. Jack O'Brien."

"Okay, yeah, O'Brien. Right." The man looked over at me then back at my father.

"Speak freely," my father said.

Tom Mitchell nodded. "So, guess he wasn't guilty after all."

"That's right."

"Well, it's been on my mind."

My father sat calmly in his chair. The radio mumbled in the background.

"You see," said Mitchell, "right after they found her, down by the river, my father passed away—over in Pocatello. So I was gone for quite a spell, you know, for the funeral and cleaning up family business and all." He rubbed a hand over his mouth and chin. "So by the time I got back, they had this here O'Brien in jail and the makings of a solid case against him. Seemed that way, then, anyway."

"Yes, that was the feeling by most folks at the time," my father said.

"Yeah, well that's the way I felt, too—then. They had the right guy, and I went back to running my taxi. Being gone that long had put a real crimp in my cash flow, so my mind was on making up for lost time. And that's where I left it, too, until it came out that they let that fella go after all."

I was standing next to my father's chair. Without looking at me, he reached out and touched my arm and motioned me to go sit down. Tom Mitchell went on.

"Don't quite know where to go with this, Mr. Wade, that's why I decided to come to you." He raised his drowsy eyelids. "I don't want to make a fool of myself, you know."

"About what, Mr. Mitchell?"

Tom Mitchell sat up straight and folded his arms across his chest. "Well, after they let that fella out of jail, I began thinking back on that night. The night they found the woman down on River Drive."

"May twenty-third."

"Yeah, May twenty-third. You see, I had a call out on Resort Street. A regular. Every Sunday night, I took this guy to the train station to catch the Union Pacific heading west to Portland. Works for the railroad, a brakeman. Still do it. Anyhow, on the way to pick him up, I see what turns out to be that Dugan woman's car."

"You mean the Hudson?"

"Yeah, that's right. A brown Hudson."

"Really? What time would that have been?"

"Oh, I'd say right at 9:15 or 9:20 that night on the way to pick up my fare. Had to be then, because that's when I always picked the guy up."

My father was resting his elbows on the arms of the chair and propping his chin on clasped hands. "And you never told the police about this?"

"Nope, I never did. I mean, it didn't seem important, not since they had arrested this guy. But now I think it maybe could mean something." Tom Mitchell looked directly at my father. "Especially, since that ain't all I saw."

My father lowered his arms and sat forward. "What else?"

Tom Mitchell licked his thin lips. "I seen another car as I was heading over to the station with my fare."

"Wait." My father sat up and held up both hands. "Don't say anything else. I have been involved with this legal stuff just enough to know that if you tell me anything, I could be called to testify about what was said to me."

The man looked confused. "Really? But what should I do?"

My father looked at Tom Mitchell; he was thinking. "Well, you need to tell the authorities about this—I mean just in case it really means something. But my advice is that you have someone else along that knows the routine."

"You mean like a lawyer or something?"

"Like a lawyer. Yes."

Oscar Doolittle was still up listening to the election returns when my father called. He agreed to see Tom Mitchell the next morning. By that time it was near midnight, and we gave up on the election. The outcome wouldn't be known until the next day, anyway. And while my father was convinced of Dewey's ultimate victory, he had been distracted; Katherine Dugan was back in our house.

The next morning was a political disaster for my father. The nation was shocked. Underdog Harry S. Truman had pulled it off. On KBKR, the national news broadcast reverberated: "Scrappy, underrated Harry Truman has captured the presidential election in one of the biggest upsets in America's political history." My father snapped off the radio and ate his breakfast in silence. That evening the *Democrat-Herald's* headlines blurted it all over again. On top of that, Baker County also went for Truman, 3035 votes to 2841. On November 3, 1948, there was no joy at 1440.

-23-

In the fall of 1948, the Dugan murder still hung like an anchor around law enforcement in Baker City, especially for T. C. Wingate. Like Truman, Wingate was thought to be a sure loser in his bid to be re-elected as district attorney. The same group of businessmen that had put up the $5,000 reward for an arrest and conviction in the teacher's death were backing their own candidate for district attorney. The face of Clarence Hotchkiss, a full-faced bald headed man, was seen everywhere smiling out from posters, billboards, and newspaper advertisements above: *Hotchkiss for D. A.* But, like Truman, T. C. Wingate squeaked out a narrow victory. Apparently, there were more voters who thought like my mother and Ruth Stillman. Again, my father was not pleased.

A week after the election, the re-elected district attorney reluctantly agreed to meet with Oscar Doolittle on a matter of some importance. Two days later, the police let it be known that they were pursuing a new lead in the Dugan killing. Shortly thereafter, Wingate called a press conference declaring the new lead to be a break in the case. The district attorney earned headlines in the paper for a week running when his lead was tied to an actual witness. The witness was Tom Mitchell, the cab owner who had sat in our living room on election eve. He was quoted as saying exactly what he had told my father, all about seeing Katherine Dugan's brown Hudson. But what really caused a stir was Mitchell's statement that he had seen a second car near River Drive. Wingate let it be known that the police were looking into that possibility, but any description of the second car, or details about the driver, remained confidential.

Wingate's political opponents, smarting from their election loss, questioned the validity of a witness who was coming forth at such a late date. The police gave the same reason that the cab driver had given to my father—about the family emergency and being out of town.

As it turned out, the Eight-0 Taxi driver was right.

While Wingate and the police department were milking the "break-in-the-case" story for all it was worth, they were tying knots in the second car story until it couldn't unravel. When they had the witness and the lead crimped down tight, Police Chief Wisdom moved. It turned out that the second car was identified as a coupe. A blue coupe. A Chevrolet.

On an overcast Saturday afternoon, Chief Wisdom swooped down on Wendell Grier's house, arrest warrant in hand, only to find his wife home alone. The story that came out later left Wisdom red-faced amidst charges of incompetence. Mrs. Grier had openly told the police where her husband was—giving a private voice lesson. But in their haste, the police roared off leaving Opal Grier in shock, and in her alarm she innocently called Wendell Grier wailing about the police knocking at their door.

By the time Chief Wisdom and two officers rang the doorbell at the Peterson home, Wendell Grier and his blue Chevrolet were gone. An all-points bulletin was put out, KBKR issued urgent bulletins, and the manhunt was on. The blue coupe seemed to vanish, and Chief Wisdom took a beating in the newspaper and on the radio. Even with the state police and county sheriffs' departments in on the chase, Grier had disappeared.

It was amazing. Wendell Grier, our choir director, the man who had elbowed me in his cramped Chevy coupe and breathed his sour breath on me, had been accused of killing the teacher and was on the run. The man who had stood face to face with my father and said Jack O'Brien's guilt was a certainty. I couldn't believe it at first; no one could. Baker City was in shock. Baker City was in a rage. Herb Gaskill's nasal urgency shifted with ease; after months of absolute certainty over Jack O'Brien's guilt, he picked up on a new murder suspect like he knew it all along.

Our phone rang again and again; I heard half-conversations: *Yes, I know, It's awful,* and *I can't believe it.*

My mother went right on playing the piano at church during the time Wendell Grier was on the run, and one of the women in the choir, a Bernice somebody, directed. Members of the congregation either went mum on the subject of Grier or gathered in two's or three's and spoke hushed words. Mr. Twiggle, once so righteous in condemning Jack O'Brien, wouldn't look my father in the eye. My father never said a word about Wendell Grier at church or anywhere else.

It would take three weeks before Wendell Grier was pulled over for a minor traffic violation in Missoula, Montana. Grier was extradited to Baker City amid great fanfare, and Chief Wisdom made sure he appeared in news photos with the handcuffed suspect. Grier's wife hired Haskin MacHall to represent her husband. That made little difference, for late on the third day after his capture, Wendell Grier confessed.

My parents stood before the radio as if it were a wise man and absorbed the sketchy details. My mother cupped an elbow in one hand and held the other hand against her mouth. After listening, my father took his hands out of his pockets, turned to his wife, and took her in his arms.

≈✿

Grier had been having an affair with Katherine Dugan for over six months prior to her death. She was a bright, pretty woman who hungered for companionship after going through a hateful divorce. Her affair with Grier came out of her loneliness and isolation.

That Sunday night, May 23, Katherine Dugan agreed to meet Grier one more time with the intention of ending the affair for good. She left the Pierce Apartments and drove her Hudson down Resort Street to River Drive. In Wendell Grier's confessional accounting, Katherine Dugan was adamant: *It's over, I can't do this anymore. Stop, Wendell, just stop. If I have to, I will confess our disgrace to Opal.* The loss of his obsession crosshatched with being exposed was too much. They argued passionately and, in the cooling evening air, Grier lost all control and beat his obsession to death in a fit of rejection and fear of revelation. Quelling his panic, he collected himself, left her there, and drove calmly away from River Drive, passing a taxi cab on his way. He took little notice of the car with Eight-0 painted on its side.

My mother was horrified. She couldn't believe that someone she knew, someone she had seen week after week, supposedly someone of faith, could be responsible for such a grievous act. But what really tore at her was remembering Wendell Grier's calm demeanor following the murder—continuing to direct the choir and conduct himself as a righteous person in spite of his great sin. She also recalled clearly, and angrily, how he had tried to get her to

193

convince her husband that he was doing the wrong thing in defending Jack O'Brien.

Mrs. Grier was a person who had seemed not to exist in a way. She was quiet, shy, and undistinguished in appearance or action. She was known only as Mrs. Grier or Wendell's wife, not as Opal, not as her own person. I remembered seeing her around the church, but only as movement, and paleness, and space filled. With Wendell Grier's arrest, Opal Grier became a real person; in her torment, she became visible. She escaped anonymity, and a life of bullying and anger. She saw her husband once in jail before putting their home up for sale and moving to Portland to live with an older sister, where she put a childless marriage on the shelf.

≈✿

One week after Wendell Grier's arrest, Arthur Woodhull died of a heart attack while attending a funeral directors conference in Portland. He was brought back to Baker City, and Sarah Woodhull asked my father to handle preparations and direct the services.

Within three weeks, Sarah Woodhull had closed a deal to sell the mortuary. The Leland Corporation, owner of 15 funerals homes in the northwest, took over operations. My father was offered a position if he wished to remain; working for the larger company would offer greater opportunity. He and my mother talked it over, then we all sat down around the kitchen table. Table talk. My father spoke about the death of Arthur Woodhull and told us again that Mrs. Woodhull had sold the mortuary and that while the new owners had offered him a job, he and our mother had decided he would not continue at the mortuary. We would be moving again.

All the talk aside, I already knew we would leave Baker City, because my mother wanted to. Not long after Wendell Grier was arrested, I was at my nightly listening post and heard my mother flatly tell my father, "I cannot stay here. Not now." There was no argument from the other side of the bed.

Two weeks before Christmas my father did reject the job offer and accepted two weeks severance pay from the Leland Corporation. In January, my father accepted a job offer from a funeral home in Tillamook, Oregon, and we moved again; another town, another mortuary.

Epilogue

In the early spring of 1949, we learned of another amazing chapter being played out in Baker City. It reminded us of all that had happened to our family there. In late March, barely a month after Wendell Grier was convicted and sentenced to life in prison, there was a break in the Lilly Marks murder case. As with the taxi driver, a witness unknown at the time of the killing came forward. This time, the witness wanted immunity for what he knew. Chief Wisdom and T. C. Wingate could hardly contain themselves. Their image as a crime-busting tandem had become the stuff of banner headlines.

The duo went silent on the Marks case while they, again, substantiated every detail of their case before saying a word. They knew full well that their political adversaries were poised to pounce on any blunder, but they needn't have worried. During their silence, the radio station and the newspaper kept Baker City residents on the edge of their seats, rehashing the city's most recently solved murder and speculating on the Mark's case.

On a cool Tuesday morning in March, with traces of snow still on the ground, Wisdom and Wingate called a press conference to announce the arrests of Frank and Presley Purdue in the Lilly

Marks murder case. My parents and I were astounded when the witness turned out to be Lenny Paris. Paris, my hero turned villain, the Power Wagon warrior of Reservoir Hill and the offender of 1440.

The Purdue brothers killed Lilly Marks at random. The three of them had been out drinking and were driving around town late one Saturday night looking for something outrageous to do, when they saw Lilly Marks walking alone on First Street. The way Lenny Paris told it, the Purdue brothers jumped out of his car and approached the woman. At the time, friends of Lilly Marks had told the police that she was probably out walking off her chronic insomnia, as she frequently did. Lilly Marks tried to fight off her assailants. The brothers dragged her into a parking lot and attempted to rape her. In the struggle, she fell striking her head and began bleeding profusely. In a panic, the Purdues and Paris sped off leaving the unconscious woman to slowly bleed to death. Frank and Presley threatened to kill Lenny if he ever told anyone.

The part he played in Lilly Marks' murder played on Lenny Paris' mind. Maybe that's why he attacked our yard. Maybe he thought my father was protecting a killer—as was he. So when the cab driver came forward and helped solve a heinous crime, he could no longer hold back. The Purdue brothers were in jail, and T. C. Wingate had gone from goat to crime crusader. On top of that, the cab driver received the $5,000 reward from the very group of businessmen who wanted to replace Wingate.

≋✲

For the Wades, 1948 finally ended. Yet the residue of that year has lived on and still resonates with me. I don't know if my parents ever resolved their differences over Jack O'Brien. I don't know if my life, or my brother's life, was distorted because of what we saw and participated in. For much of what I remember, I am proud. I'll always remember my father, an ordinary man fighting for someone he felt was being wronged. I know he never rid himself of the ghost of Warney Webster.

I remember my mother's strength. She did what she felt she had to do—challenging, holding back, loving. She never served as a church pianist again, even though she continued to play her piano at home. The day we read in the paper about Wendell Grier being sent to prison, I remember finding her in her bedroom sitting on the edge of the bed, crying. Her body was turned, so she didn't see me. Her shoulders rose and fell with deep sobs; her grief was intense, then over. She never spoke of the man again.

My parents came away from that year with internal scars neither deserved, and that would never go away. The true test was the remainder of their years together. They did love each other and were strong for their sons. I watched them provide and care for us and acknowledge their commitment to each other, but I think the light went out of their passion for one another that year in Baker City. It saddened me that they would not see what they had become.

They are both gone now. My mother passed first from the same kind of cancer her mother had. David and I sat at her bedside at the end and watched her smile in great pain. My father wasn't there; he couldn't do it. They had said goodbye at another time.

Before my father died, he finally told me why he fought so hard for Jack O'Brien: *They never let me visit Warney in jail. Only his parents. So I did a stupid thing. I called the dead girl's mother and pleaded with her that Warney wasn't the one that killed her daughter. The next day, the paper had a front page story about how friends of the accused had begged the mother to spare him from ex-*

ecution. I called Warney's folks and told them that wasn't what I'd said. But it didn't matter, Warney really believed he was going to die. He didn't wait. I caused that, Philip. I couldn't allow it to happen again. But Jack O'Brien didn't cleanse me of my guilt. Nothing ever will.

≡✿

I've tried to discuss what happened with David, but it never works. He's heard the story, of course, but my brother was too young to really know what was going on. When we talk about 1948 today, he hears it all as if he weren't there. Maybe that's good.

As for me, it remains an indelible year. I was just the right age for all of what happened to enter my mind uncluttered. It was a cram course in adult behavior. Some of it horrible. Some of it noble. Most of it, just doing the best one can.

≡✿

Above: George Wright
with his mother El-
eanor Wright. Circa
1949 in Baker City.

Right: George
Wright, 2005.

Author Bio

A native Oregonian, George Byron Wright was born on the Columbia River at The Dalles, Oregon. Along with his mother and brother, he migrated to three other small Oregon towns as his father pursued the life of a mortician. Living in Baker City, Tillamook and Roseburg endowed him with a lifelong fondness for small places.

During a lengthy career in the not-for-profit sector, George wrote professionally, publishing books on management and board development. He also wrote a newspaper column for several years and operated a retail bookstore. With the publication of *Baker City 1948*, his lifelong passion for writing fiction merges with his own micropublishing company—C3 Publications. This is his first published novel.

George lives with his wife and first reader, Betsy, in Portland, Oregon.

ORDER MORE COPIES OF THIS BOOK, AND OTHER TITLES FROM C3 PUBLICATIONS

FICTION TITLES

Baker City 1948

In Baker City, Oregon in 1948, nine-year-old Philip Wade faces adult realities over the violent death of a local school-teacher and his father's surprising defense of the accused.

NONFICTION TITLES

BEYOND NOMINATING: A GUIDE TO GAINING AND SUSTAINING SUCCESSFUL NOT-FOR-PROFIT BOARDS

This popular manual is a road map to attracting the competent, talented, and visionary volunteer leadership every not-for-profit organization wants and needs. Learn how to assess, plan, and effectively recruit the best board leadership. Includes 25 forms, model documents, worksheets and guidelines to help make each step easier. Written by former not-for-profit executive, George B. Wright, who applies his nearly 40 years of experience in the volume. ISBN 0-9632655-1-2, 87 pages, paper, $25.00+S&H.

THE NOT-FOR-PROFIT CEO: A SURVIVOR'S MANUAL

Before you recruit another board member, raise another dollar, or prepare your next budget, read this book. In today's environment of increasing scrutiny and competition, it's critical to apply the author's six management checkpoints: 1) Managing a Democracy, 2) Search & Deploy, 3) Relate, Relate, Facilitate, 4) Dollars In, Dollars Out, 5) Out and About, and 6) Wide Angle Lens. A Valuable refresher for veteran NFP CO's, a guidebook for the new CEO, and a view through the looking glass for future CEOs. ISBN 0-96322655-0-4, 138 pages, paper, $11.95+S&H. By George B. Wright

See the next page for ordering information.

COPY THIS ORDER FORM

NOTE: Order our books through your local bookstore, on our website, or by completing this form and mailing your payment using check or money order.

Quantity	Amount
.... *Baker City 1948* ($13.95)	....
.... *Beyond Nominating* ($25)	....
.... *The Not-For-Profit CEO* ($11.95)	....
Total Amount of Order	....
Shipping & handling	....
(add $2.50 for 1st book and $1.50 for each add'l book)	
TOTAL PAYMENT ENCLOSED	$ ....

Name ....

Address ....

City/State/Zip ....

Phone ....

Email ....

Send Mail Orders to: C3 Publications
3495 NW Thurman St.
Portland, OR 97210
Voice:503-223-0268
Fax: 503-223-3083
georgec3pub@comcast.net

Order now from our website: www.c3publications.com

Colophon

The text of this book is set in Adobe's Minion Pro Condensed (OTF), 11.5/16. Minion Pro was designed by Robert Slimbach. As the foundry notes: "The first version of Minion was released in 1990. Cyrillic additions were released in 1992, and finally the OpenType Pro version was released in 2000. Minion Pro is inspired by classical, old style typefaces of the late Renaissance, a period of elegant, beautiful, and highly readable type designs. Minion Pro combines the aesthetic and functional qualities that make text type highly readable with the versatility of OpenType digital technology."

Titling and folios are in Harting Regular (PostScript) designed by David Rakowski in 1992 as shareware. It is now commercially distributed by Intecsas, a digital foundry based in Düsseldorf, Germany.